PLAYING GAMES

"Of course I'll come to the pep rally" Lori promised Nick. "I'm still your number-one fan, aren't I?" she asked, teasing him.

"Always." Nick laughed and gave her a quick kiss.

Lori could see the concern in his eyes. She knew they were both worried about the same thing. She was crazy about Nick, and she couldn't bear to see his friends lose faith in him—especially because of her. If she had to go to the Atwood pep rally on Friday night to help him stay in tight with his teammates, then she'd do it.

But I sure hope no one from Merivale finds out!

Merivale Mall

PLAYING GAMES

by Jana Ellis

Troll Associates

Library of Congress Cataloging-in-Publication Data

Ellis, Jana.
    Playing games / by Jana Ellis.
        p.   cm.—(Merivale mall; #3)
    Summary: Sixteen-year-old Lori finds her loyalties divided when
her school's football team faces a crucial game against a rival team
on which her boyfriend is star quarterback.
    ISBN 0-8167-1358-8 (pbk.)
    [1. Interpersonal relations—Fiction. 2. High Schools—Fiction.
3. Schools—Fiction.] I. Title. II. Series: Ellis, Jana.
Merivale mall; #3.
PZ7.E472Pl   1989
[Fic]—dc19   88-12389

A TROLL BOOK, published by Troll Associates,
Mahwah, NJ 07430

Copyright © 1989 by Troll Associates, Mahwah, New Jersey

Printed in the United States of America.

10 9 8 7 6 5 4 3 2 1

PLAYING GAMES

CHAPTER ONE

OOMPH! His guard went down hard. Now what could he do? Jack Baxter, the quarterback for the Merivale Vikings, wondered. He was completely unprotected. He had to get rid of the ball within the next few seconds or he'd be down too. Only a minute to the final gun. Where was that receiver? There, to the right. *Darn!* That bozo safety had just come out of nowhere to cover him.

Jack stepped to the right and hoped to lose the linebacker, who was sticking like glue. Those Westwood guys sure knew how to cover. He'd have to run with it! He'd take two more steps to the right to fake out that big sucker of a linebacker.

A quick turn to the left. There. That got him off his tail. *Okay, now, feet, do your stuff. Oh, no!* Where did that cornerback come from? Jack tucked the ball against his left side and straight-armed him out of the way. Thank heavens he was little. Jack looked up and couldn't believe it—he had a clear run to the goal! Thirty feet more. Twenty. Where was everyone? His teammates must be knocking down the opposition Westwood players like dominoes. Ten feet. Almost there . . .

Gina Nichols leapt into the air in a perfect split jump as her quarterback boyfriend cleared the goal line. He'd done it! The score was 13 to 7—and there was the final gun! Merivale had beaten Westwood. Now on to their chief rival, Atwood Academy.

Gina led the rest of the cheerleaders in one final victory whoop before following the fans onto the field. Pushing through the Merivale crowd to get to Jack, Gina was almost swallowed up.

Jack had been lifted high on a teammate's shoulders and had to lean way over to kiss his petite girlfriend on top of her shiny strawberry blond hair, which was pulled up into a high ponytail. When he bent down, he said in a loud whisper, "Later, babe!"

She grinned back, her large brown eyes shining with unshed tears. Her sister cheerleaders hugged her, and then they all did a victory dance in a circle around her and Jack. Their black and red outfits moved in a blur of color.

He did it, Gina thought. Jack had only to take on that Nick Hobart, the quarterback for the

Atwood Cougars. Twenty years of hope at Merivale would find its reward in that game in two weeks. Merivale had never beaten Atwood in all that time. Now the two best quarterbacks in the league would be pitted against each other. *But Jack will do it. He has to. He just has to!* Gina thought.

In the third row of the bleachers, sixteen-year-old Lori Randall was standing and digging into her handbag. Since it was Friday night, she might see her boyfriend—Nick Hobart, Atwood's quarterback—later, so she removed the Merivale High button that said "Merivale is #1!" and stuck it into her bag, all the time pretending to grope for her car keys.

She quietly gasped as she glanced up and caught her friend, Patsy Donovan, starting up the bleachers to rejoin her after deserting the mob on the field. Lori hoped Patsy hadn't seen her put the button away. But because Lori was a blond, she blushed and colored so easily that Patsy would probably guess that something had happened anyway.

"Go-o-o-o Merivale, beat Atwood. Go-o-o-o Merivale, beat Atwood," Patsy chanted. She looked up into the face of her beautiful friend. "Say, Lor, what is it? Are you okay?"

"Why shouldn't I be okay? We just beat Westwood, didn't we?" Lori hadn't meant to sound so harsh. Reluctant to meet her friend's gaze and tell her the truth, she looked down at the toe of her black leather boot, and her long blond hair fell like a curtain and hid her face. Then she looked up again and joined in the chanting, which now had a hushed and almost reverential quality as it swept over the entire stadium and field. She felt terrible for speaking so meanly to Patsy and turned to smile shyly at her.

Her chubby friend linked arms with Lori, and they swayed and chanted with everyone else.

"Hi, guys. What a mob scene down there," Ann Larson said, joining her friends. She tousled Patsy's curly reddish brown hair and put her arm around her waist. "It's really working," she said to Patsy, referring to Patsy's new diet.

Patsy's hazel eyes glowed as she took in the compliment. She had only lost ten pounds so far, but she was losing it sensibly with a nonfad diet and plenty of exercise.

The three friends started down the stairs to join the crowd as it slowly moved out of the bright lights of the stadium and into the dark of the clear autumn evening. With Patsy in the middle, they linked arms so that from the rear the three looked like a sandwich cookie with the taller girls on the outside. Ann's wavy, chestnut-colored hair hung down her back, swinging back and forth like a metronome keeping time as she walked.

Looking over at Lori, Ann noticed that she didn't have her button on. "Hey, where's your button?" Ann asked.

"Don't know. It must have fallen off," Lori lied, still unable to tell them the truth.

"I just happen to have an extra one. Here," Ann said as she pulled one out of the giant satchel she used as a handbag.

"Thanks."

"We need all the spirit we can get to beat Atwood in two weeks. Well, aren't you going to put it on?" she asked, not understanding Lori's hesitation.

"In a minute," Lori said, fudging.

"Okay, Lor. What gives?" Patsy yanked on Lori's arm and confronted her directly.

"I guess I can't keep anything from you two. I know it sounds silly," Lori finally blurted out. "But every time I put on this button, I feel disloyal to Nick."

Lori felt a whole lot better after she had said it out loud. Her friends looked sympathetic. Lori should have remembered that she could always count on them.

"Sorry, Lor. I didn't even think of Nick," Ann said.

"Gee, that *is* hard," Patsy agreed. "He *is* the guy that Merivale loves to hate during the football season. Oh, well, at least you have a boyfriend. And what a boyfriend! An Adonis."

Lori nodded her head and smiled, agreeing.

Nick was pretty special—to say nothing of handsome. Six foot one inches tall, slim, muscular, with golden brown hair and aquamarine eyes. When they had first met, Lori thought she wouldn't have a chance with him. After all, he *was* Nick Hobart, all-around hunk at Atwood Academy, a private prep school where only the wealthiest families sent their kids.

"Okay, Lori, why the grin?" Ann asked.

"Oh, was I grinning?" she replied, her mouth still curving softly. "I was just thinking about Nick and the first time we met. You know, he really is worth any trouble he may cause me. Did I ever tell you guys exactly how we met?"

"Gee, Lor, I don't think so. Was it at the mall, maybe? Were you on a break from Tio's Tacos, and standing looking into a fountain?" Patsy asked, wide-eyed with innocence.

"And did Nick save you from a maniac kid on a skateboard? Pulling you away just before the kid was going to knock you into the fountain? Gosh, I don't think I've ever heard that story. Have you, Patsy?" Ann asked, mirroring Patsy's innocent mask.

"Sorry about that. Guess you've heard it, huh?" Lori said.

"Not more than ten or twelve times. Do you want to tell us again?"

"That's it!" Lori said, shaking her fist. She took after her two friends, who had separated and run away from her in opposite directions.

Eventually they all met in the parking lot beside Lori's car. None of them could say a word because they were laughing and gasping for air.

"Come on, you guys, let's go home," Lori finally said, dangling the keys to her new used car in front of them.

"Really, Lori, we do understand. It is going to be hard for you, dating Atwood's quarterback. Both our teams will be unbelievably psyched to win. The game is going to be all anyone talks about for days," Ann said.

"Well, I'm not going to be put in the position of having to choose between Nick and Merivale High. I do want the Vikings to win, but I also want Nick to win!"

"Maybe you should start taking classes over at Atwood. You obviously don't feel a shred of loyalty for Merivale," said Gina Nichols, strolling out of the dark shadows and into the glare of a car's headlights. Obviously Gina had been listening in on Lori's conversation with Ann and Patsy.

"Come on, Gina. That's not true and you know it," Lori calmly replied. Gina's words made her angry, but she controlled her temper. She knew it was best to avoid any confrontation with Gina that involved loyalty to the Vikings or Jack Baxter, in particular.

"Lori doesn't have to prove anything to you, Gina," Ann said in her friend's defense.

The pretty cheerleader just glared at Ann, trying to stare her down. Gina was acting the part of Merivale's and Jack's avenging angel.

"Well, why isn't she wearing a button? And, Lori, I don't see a single bumper sticker on your car," she added in her loud, piercing voice. "I guess Nick Hobart wouldn't approve. Well, what's it going to be? Nick or us?" She had been steadily raising her tone until she was practically shouting.

All around them, engines were quickly turned off, and the parking lot became eerily quiet. Lori could picture everyone peering out from their darkened cars, listening, and waiting to see what would happen. If she put the button on, she *would* feel disloyal to Nick. But if she didn't, she'd feel disloyal to her school. The only sound in the lot was of engines ticking as they cooled down. Lori finally decided. She'd put on the button and end this silly confrontation.

She reached into her bag and picked it out. "There, it's on," she announced flatly. "Will that do?"

"I guess we'll have to see," Gina said huffily. Just then an arm reached out and circled her slim waist, drawing her back.

"So, what do you say? Let's go celebrate." Jack Baxter had just walked up to them and now stood holding Gina back against his powerful body. "Leave it, babe," he whispered into her ear. "Hobart and I will settle it on the field."

Gina started to move off with him then. But suddenly she stopped and turned. "Here are a few bumper stickers for your car, Lori. Don't forget your locker either," she added as a parting shot.

Engines were clicked on and revved up. Then the headlights came on. Loud war whoops sounded throughout the lot as cars peeled away, their tires screeching.

"The unbelievable nerve of some people!" Ann said, fuming. "Who does she think she is?"

"Yeah, she sure could use a few lessons at charm school, if you ask me," Patsy said.

"Forget it, guys," Lori said. "It's bad enough that I'm on Gina's hit list. You don't have to be in on it too. Ever since she heard I was going out with Nick, she's acted like there's a competition between us. Just because we're both going out with quarterbacks, she seems to think we should be rivals too."

"Gina's a jerk," Patsy said simply. "She thinks she runs the whole school."

"The sad thing is that kids *really* listen to her." Ann shook her head. "You'd better watch out, Lori. Gina can make your life miserable if she wants to. Remember what happened to Sheryl Dobson?" Ann asked, naming another cheerleader. "Gina thought Sheryl had her eye on Jack, so she started spreading all kinds of rumors about her, and a lot of people believed her—even Sheryl's closest friends! She didn't leave her house for weeks. When Gina goes after somebody, she doesn't fool around."

"Let's just hope she doesn't go after me," Lori said and tried to smile. She picked up the stickers and plastered one on the front bumper of her car.

CHAPTER TWO

After school the next Monday, Lori, Ann, and Patsy drove to work at the Merivale Mall in Lori's car. Lori loved the car—a red Triumph Spitfire she'd bought at an incredibly low price. Nick sometimes teased her that she fussed over her car more than she fussed over him—even though they *both* knew that wasn't true.

But Lori didn't feel as if she had been very kind to her car when she plastered the bumper sticker on it. She had been afraid that Gina Nichols would patrol the school parking lot, and any car without a sticker might end up with flat tires—or worse. Ann and Patsy both agreed that she was better safe than sorry with Gina.

Once they arrived at the mall, the three girls separated: Ann to the Body Shoppe, a fitness salon on the third level, where she was an aerobics instructor; Patsy to Cookie Connection, a shop that sold cookies and ice cream; and Lori to Tio's Tacos, a Mexican restaurant owned by a man named Ernie Goldbloom.

As long as they had to work, the girls were happy to be at Merivale Mall, a brand-new chrome-and-glass confection. Just to walk in through the soundless doors would start most people fantasizing about shopping sprees. The central, domed skylight filtered natural sunshine down on the huge plants on each of the four levels. The lower level had bubbling fountains and massive stone benches set among the greenery. The whole floor resembled an oasis, restful and lush.

At Tio's, Lori quickly changed into the uniform she thoroughly despised. It was an orange nylon dress covered with a bright yellow apron that said "Tio's Tacos! Muchos Buenos!" in large black letters. Lori had hopes of becoming a fashion designer someday, so wearing this hideous uniform was absolutely devastating. But since she needed the job to save money for college, she tried her best to ignore it. After pulling her hair back in a big clip, Lori reached for her "Merivale is #1!" button, but couldn't quite bring herself to pin it on.

I'm bound to see loads of kids from school, Lori decided. *So, here goes.* She jabbed the pin into her dress. *No, wait. Nick's just across the concourse. He'll see it.* Carefully, she backed the pin

out, hoping it wouldn't snag her nylon uniform. Nick's father's store, Hobart Electronics,
was directly across from Tio's, and when Nick
worked there they managed to steal a bit of
time for each other.

I do want the Vikings to win, Lori thought,
trying to thread the stupid pin back into the
same holes in her dress. *But—when I think of
Nick, I feel rotten.* Yanking it off for the last time,
Lori looked down and saw a long thread leading out from a giant pucker!

Lori threw the button across the room and
decided not to think about it another second.
She quickly checked her reflection, and then at
the last second picked up the dumb pin, shoved
it in her pocket, and ran out to the counter.

As Lori walked into the restaurant, she heard
the unmistakable sound of Gina Nichols's voice
filling the space. Acting on sheer survival in-
stinct, Lori darted behind the milkshake ma-
chine and jabbed her button on once again. Just
in time! Gina was waiting for her.

"Well, if it isn't Lori Randall!" Gina said with
mock surprise. "The girl with the *most* school
spirit." The cheerleader glanced back over her
shoulder to snicker with her friends. "*Love* your
button, Lori," Gina said, taunting her.

"Glad you approve." Lori looked Gina right
in the eye. "Listen, Gina, I go to Merivale, and
that's where my loyalties are. Just because I
date a guy from Atwood doesn't mean that

that would change! If you don't believe me,
then that's just tough," she said quietly and a
little too calmly.

For once, Gina was shocked speechless. And
before she could think of anything to say, Lori's
boss, Ernie Goldbloom, appeared. "Listen, miss,"
he said brusquely to Gina, "if you don't want to
order anything, step aside. You're holding up
the line. Next please."

Lori watched as the cheerleader's face turned
beet red. But Gina finally did step aside without
saying another word.

Score one for me, Lori said to herself. She took
an order and sent a Styrofoam plate of tacos
across the counter. When Lori looked up, Gina
and her friends had paraded out of the restaurant. She breathed a sigh of relief.

Later, Lori was sitting on a bench outside of
Tio's on her break. She caught sight of a small
group of Cougar football players. They were all
wearing their navy wool and white leather jack-
ets. They'd obviously just come from football
practice.

At the very center of the group, walking with
a graceful lope, was Nick Hobart. *Her* Nick Hobart! She still couldn't believe they were dating.
Nick was talking to a friend, so he didn't see
Lori.

Watching him, Lori noticed how easily he
joked with his friends. Lori felt her heart leap—
suddenly it was difficult to draw a deep breath.

She realized with a start that she was sitting in the middle of the mall, grinning like an idiot—and she didn't even care.

What she really wanted to do was run up to him and brush her hand through his thick golden brown hair, but she forced herself to remain where she was.

There! He finally caught her eye, and broke into a grin that matched hers. Still smiling, his eyes glowing, he quickened his pace and walked over to her well ahead of his friends.

"Hi, Nick!" Lori stood up to greet him.

He swooped her up in a giant bear hug, practically swinging her off her feet. "So—how goes it?" Nick asked, his arm still slung around her shoulder.

Lori laughed. "Great, now that you're here."

"Hey, what's this?" he asked, pointing at her "Merivale is #1!" button.

"A few Merivale cheerleaders came into Tio's before and I had to put it on. They think anyone who *doesn't* wear one is a traitor," she said lightly.

Nick laughed. "People are really getting crazy about this game."

"Some people are really going overboard if you ask me," Lori said. She slipped her arm around Nick and gave him a quick squeeze. "I think we're going to have to put up with a lot of grief in the next two weeks."

"Hey, let them say whatever they want. Who

cares?" Nick said, smiling down at her. "No football game is going to get me, or you, bent out of shape—no way."

Lori smiled too. Nick always understood. They could talk about things without hiding their real feelings. That was one of the reasons she liked him so much.

"Right," Lori replied, squeezing him again. She did reach up and slide the button off though. "How was practice today?"

Nick looked down. "Could have been better—"

"What happened?"

"I screwed up a few plays. I kept missing the open receivers," Nick explained. "Guess my timing was off, and I had a bad day. It happens."

"You have plenty of time before—" Lori started to say.

But before she could finish, one of Nick's teammates, a burly fullback, stepped up to them. "No wonder you had such a bad day today, Hobart. I forgot your girlfriend goes to Merivale." He tried to pretend it was a joke by smiling, but Lori knew he was serious.

"Yeah, that's right—" another Cougar agreed. "She does go to Merivale." He didn't even try to soften his attack.

"Hey, cool it, guys," Nick said. "I had an off day today—that's all. It doesn't make any difference where Lori and I go to school. I play my best for the Cougars, no matter what."

"Okay, man," the heavyset Cougar agreed.

"But it'd be easier if we knew your girl was for you all the way—"

"My girl's name is Lori. You know that. And you can call her by her name."

"Of course I'm for him," Lori said, speaking up. How could this clown accuse her of not being for him?

"Well, I think he could use some heavy-duty cheering from his girl—excuse me—from Lori," the other one said. "Friday night there's a big pep rally at Atwood. Maybe you could plan to be there. What do you say—*Lori*?" he asked, challenging her.

Lori looked up at Nick. Could his team possibly be losing confidence in him? And all because of her? Lori would never let that happen in a million years.

"Of course I'll come to the pep rally," she said brightly. "I wouldn't miss it for anything."

"You heard what she said, guys. Now do me a favor and disappear."

The guys slowly walked away, heading for Cookie Connection. "Thanks for helping me out, Lori. They're not really bad guys. They're just psyched for the game." Nick shook his head, a lock of hair falling across his forehead. "You understand, don't you?"

"Sure, I understand, Nick," Lori said. "Besides, I want to go to the rally. I'm still your number-one fan, aren't I?" she asked, teasing him.

"Always." Nick laughed and gave her a quick kiss.

Lori could see the concern in his eyes. She knew they were both worried about the same thing. The next two weeks were going to be difficult.

But she did know she was crazy about Nick, and she couldn't bear to see his friends lose faith in him—especially because of her. If she had to go to the Atwood pep rally on Friday night to help him stay in tight with his teammates, then she'd do it.

But I sure hope no one from Merivale finds out!

CHAPTER THREE

At Atwood Academy on the next Friday, the whole school was gearing up for the pep rally. Huge banners that stretched across the corridors declared, "Cougars are the Greatest!" and "Atwood is Unbeatable!" There didn't seem to be a single student who wasn't wearing navy and white, the school colors.

In Mrs. Ellis's psychology class, Danielle Sharp, Lori Randall's first cousin, fidgeted the whole period. *When will this torture be over?* she wondered, glancing down at her gold watch. She shook her head once and her glowing red hair cascaded in fiery waves around her shoulders.

Danielle was used to having things her own way, and she'd never been good at hiding boredom. She yawned out loud and tapped her perfectly manicured nails on the desk top. She couldn't wait to get home and pick out her outfit for that night's pep rally. It was a fact that she was one of the prettiest girls at Atwood. But it never hurt to make sure that no one else forgot it.

"Maybe Danielle Sharp would like to tell us something about Piaget's theory of child development?" Mrs. Ellis looked straight at Danielle, a steely glint in her pale blue eyes.

"Um—excuse me? I didn't hear the question, Mrs. Ellis. Sorry." Danielle stalled. If she could just waste a few more seconds, the bell would ring and she'd be off the hook.

Mrs. Ellis sighed and ran a hand through her short, dark hair, threaded with silvery gray strands. "We are going over last night's reading assignment, Danielle. In case you hadn't noticed—"

Muffled laughter was heard throughout the classroom. Danielle wanted to slide under her desk. *That snide witch! How dare she make everyone laugh at me!* Danielle thought angrily.

Just then the bell rang. The students hurriedly gathered their books and sprang out of their seats. "Just a second, folks—" Mrs. Ellis shouted over the confusion. "Before you stampede out of here, I want to hand back last week's exam."

The class let out a loud chorus of groans. Mrs. Ellis ignored them and began calling out names. "Connors. Siegel. Wilson—very nice, Nancy. Sharp—"

Danielle reached out and took her paper. She felt a fluttery feeling in the pit of her stomach.

She was afraid to look at her grade, but forced herself.

An F! That's impossible! I knew I didn't do a great job, but there's no way I could have flunked.

Out in the hallway, kids jostled her left and right, but Danielle hardly noticed as she walked toward her locker, lost in thought. If her parents ever found out, they would be absolutely furious—especially her father. What if he decided to punish her by taking away her charge cards and allowance, she thought with a fresh wave of terror.

Danielle shoved the test in her notebook and fought her way back through the corridor of frenzied students. Mrs. Ellis was still in her classroom, making a neat pile of her books and papers. Danielle paused a moment in the doorway, then stepped inside.

"Danielle—did you forget something?" Mrs. Ellis looked up at her.

"No—I just wanted to talk to you about the— test." Danielle looked down at her notebook a second. "I didn't do very well—"

"No, you didn't," Mrs. Ellis agreed. "Although I know you're capable of doing much better."

"Since I failed the test—does that mean I'm flunking the course?" Danielle asked nervously.

Mrs. Ellis paused. "Possibly. If you don't improve, you could."

"Please let me take the exam over, Mrs. Ellis.

I know I could do better—you just said so
yourself."

Mrs. Ellis looked sympathetic, but she shook
her head and raked her fingers through her
hair. "You know I can't let you take it over. It
wouldn't be fair to the rest of the class."

"But, Mrs. Ellis, you don't understand. I just
can't flunk this class. My dad'll hit the roof.
Isn't there *anything* I can do to bring this grade
up? What if I wrote an extra paper? Will that
help?"

Mrs. Ellis gave Danielle a long look. "If you
really want to improve your grade, I will allow
you to do an extra project. You might not want
to do it, though, when you hear what it is—"

Danielle was so relieved, she could have leaned
over and kissed Mrs. Ellis. "Are you kidding?
I'll do anything— Name it."

"I want you to volunteer fifteen hours at the
Downtown Day-Care Center."

"A day-care center?" A horrifying vision of
whining, dirty brats whirled through Danielle's
mind. The thought of all their sticky little hands
on her clothes made her feel faint.

"That's right." Mrs. Ellis looked as if she
were trying to keep from smiling at Danielle's
shocked reaction. "Fifteen hours of volunteer
work. That's the *only* way to pull up your grade.
You do like small children, don't you?"

"Oh, sure—I love little kids," Danielle fibbed,
her eyes wide open. *Mrs. Ellis is getting back at*

me for all the times I've goofed off in her class.
"When do I start?" she asked, trying to sound eager about the idea.

Mrs. Ellis gave her a rare smile. "You can start this afternoon, after your last class," she said, jotting something on a piece of paper. "Here's the address and the name of the teacher, Betsy Harper. Her afternoon help just quit, and I know she'll be thrilled to have you."

Danielle felt horrified as she picked up the sheet of paper and glanced at the address. "Thanks, Mrs. Ellis," she said as she left the classroom. "See you tomorrow."

Out in the hallway, Danielle stopped and leaned against the wall. She could have screamed at the very top of her lungs. *Fifteen hours of volunteer work with a pack of little monsters! How am I ever going to live through it?*

After her last class Danielle went to her locker and saw Heather Barron and Teresa Woods waiting for her. They looked gorgeous as usual. Danielle knew the three of them were sensational together. Heather's long black hair set off her own red waves and Teresa's thick brown mane.

"Hey, Danielle," Heather said, "dump your books and let's get out of here."

"Ready?" Teresa asked. "You are still coming over to my house this afternoon to get ready for the pep rally, aren't you?"

Oh, no! I completely forgot, Danielle thought frantically. *I'll have to come up with some excuse— and fast.*

"Gee—I can't. I have to do an errand for my mother. I've got to pick up a dress that she's having altered," Danielle hurriedly explained.

"Well, we'll come with you."

"No! I mean, I don't think so." Danielle opened her locker and pretended to rummage around in it while she thought. "It'll be boring. My mom's—uh—meeting me there. She wants me to see the dress on her."

Teresa and Heather exchanged suspicious glances. "You never mentioned this before, Danielle. What gives?" Heather asked, her blue eyes darting from Danielle to Teresa.

"Really, Danielle, you act like you're on a mission for the CIA or something," Teresa added.

"Hey, I know. I'll bet Danielle's got a new boyfriend," Heather teased in sing-song tone. "Do you, Danielle?"

Danielle was relieved that her friends had come up with a logical excuse for her odd behavior. *Let them think I'm seeing some new guy for the next few weeks. What harm'll it do? It'll give them something to gossip about.*

"I'd *love* to hang out, but—well, you know, duty calls."

"Some duty, I'll bet," Teresa said, her brown eyes narrowing as Danielle slammed her locker and ran down the hall.

*   *   *

The day-care center was located on a side street in a modest section of Merivale. Neighboring some small row houses, the older building had been painted bright yellow with white trim. There was a fenced-in playground at the side and back and a sign in front that read "Downtown Day-Care" with a colorful rainbow painted across the top.

As Danielle approached the building, she could hear the shouting, whistling, and banging of children at play. It sounded as if there were hundreds of them. She took a deep breath and slowly pushed in the door.

The center was one huge room, each of its walls painted a different pastel color. Children's drawings and paintings were taped everywhere. Open shelves along the walls held games, stuffed animals, dolls, and toys of every description. There was a puppet theater set up in one corner and a huge, walk-in playhouse in the other.

Danielle stepped inside, but no one noticed her. Led by a woman who Danielle assumed was Betsy Harper, the children were parading around the room wearing colorful paper hats. Each of them had a small instrument to play. They were banging and clanging drums and tambourines and blowing on whistles. Later, Betsy Harper explained it was called a rhythm parade. Danielle called it torture.

The noise was so deafening, she couldn't hear

herself think. *It's only fifteen hours*, she reminded herself. *It can't be that bad. . . .*

Two hours later Danielle had to admit that she had been right. It wasn't that bad—it was a *thousand* times worse than she'd imagined. She was exhausted and hoarse from trying to make herself heard over screaming toddlers and preschoolers. She had a glob of green modeling clay embedded in her hair, a hand print of red paint on her gray suede skirt, and runs in her hot pink tights.

Most of the children had been picked up, and Danielle had her first real chance to talk to Betsy, a thin and lively young woman in her midtwenties. Danielle had to admire the way Betsy handled the kids. She had endless amounts of energy and patience, and all her charges seemed to adore her.

"So, how did you like your first day, Danielle?" Betsy asked with a bright smile.

"It was—fine." She tried to force a smile. *If Betsy tells Mrs. Ellis that I'm not getting along well here, I'll be stuck with that F for sure.*

Betsy gave Danielle a knowing grin. "I know the little *darlings* are hard to keep up with at first," she said. "But you'll get the hang of it after a while. Besides—I think they really like you."

"They *like* me?" Danielle asked in disbelief. She gave up acting as if she had been enjoying herself. It was obvious that Betsy saw right through her. "Is that why they threw toys at me, stuck clay in my hair, and used my skirt for a hand towel?"

Betsy laughed, her huge, dark eyes sympathetic. "Maybe you should wear more practical clothes the next time you come," she gently suggested as she began putting toys away.

"I'll keep that in mind," Danielle said as she helped her straighten up the huge playroom.

Finally the day-care center was restored to order. The last child had been picked up by his mother. "Well—Monday is another day," Betsy said cheerfully as she shut out the lights and locked the door. "Will I see you again, Danielle?"

"Oh, don't worry. I'll be back," Danielle promised. She glanced down at the paint on her suede skirt. *Because I really have no choice!*

CHAPTER FOUR

Atwood Academy looked particularly impressive at night, Lori thought as she drove up to the school and parked that night. The main ivy-covered brick building was illuminated by giant floodlights and decorated with a huge banner across its white-columned entrance. Navy and white, the banner bore the school's prestigious crest.

She walked down a gravel path, following voices raised in a favorite Cougar fight song. In the distance, people were gathered around a huge bonfire. Everyone appeared to be dressed in Atwood colors. Each student was waving a sign.

"Cougars are Untameable!" she read on one sign. Lori glanced around to see if anyone recognized her. She honestly felt as though she were a spy, although she knew she was only there because of Nick.

*But if anybody from Merivale ever finds out I was
at an Atwood pep rally, I'm dead,* Lori thought as
she nervously glanced around. But how would
anyone find out? she told herself. If another
Merivale student were there, they certainly
couldn't tell. Nick didn't ask much of her, and
she didn't mind doing him a small favor. How
could she refuse to be part of this celebration to
wish him luck?

She hadn't yet caught sight of Nick's handsome face in the crowd, but she was eager to
show him that she was there, cheering him on
and doing all she could to convince his teammates of her support.

"Lori? What are you doing here?"

Lori spun around to see her cousin Danielle.
As usual, Danielle looked perfect. She had on a
beautiful, hand-knit Italian sweater of navy and
cream stripes.

"Shhh! Not so loud!" Lori pulled her cousin
into the shadows. "Let's go over here, away
from the crowd," she suggested.

Lori knew that Danielle was embarrassed that
she was actually related to a girl who worked
behind the counter at Tio's Tacos. Before Danielle's
dad, Lori's uncle Mike, had made money devel-
oping Merivale Mall, Danielle and Lori had been
close, almost like sisters. But once the Sharps
had moved to Wood Hollow Hills, Merivale's
most exclusive area, the girls drifted apart. They
were still friendly, but no longer best friends.

Lori knew Danielle wouldn't mind stepping out of the light of the bonfire. In that way she wouldn't be seen talking with her poor relation.

"Lori, what's wrong with you tonight?" Danielle was astounded at the behavior of her normally sane cousin.

Lori didn't usually feel comfortable confiding in Danielle. Danielle could be friendly toward her one minute, then turn on her the next. This night was special. And Lori was in enemy territory at Atwood Academy. Danielle's was the only familiar face Lori had seen so far.

"Well, I came to cheer for Nick. His teammates have been giving him grief about having a girlfriend from Merivale High. But I really don't want anyone from my school to find out I was here," Lori said in a hushed voice.

"Oh, I get it." Danielle nodded. "Don't worry, your secret's safe with me. When would I gossip—or even talk—with anyone from *your* school?"

In spite of Danielle's insult, Lori had to smile. She was safe because of her cousin's snobbery.

All of a sudden the Atwood Academy band struck up a rousing rendition of their school song. A spotlight hit the crowd, and a voice over the PA system boomed a welcome to the happy Cougar fans. Lori and Danielle moved in closer.

The Atwood cheering squad jumped up and down, waving their pom-poms. Someone dressed up in a cougar outfit did handstands and cartwheels. One by one, the players were introduced. Outfitted in full uniform, they trotted into the center of the circle and lined up in front of the bonfire.

Lori could hardly wait for Nick to be introduced. Finally she saw his smiling face appear in the spotlight, and the crowd went wild.

"And number thirty-two, that passing, running—'Mr. Right Stuff' himself—quarterback, Nick Hobart!"

Forgetting that she wasn't supposed to attract attention to herself, Lori cheered at the top of her lungs, jumping up and down with everyone else.

When the entire team had been introduced, the Atwood cheerleaders led the audience in several fight songs. Then the head coach gave a brief, but inspiring, speech. Lori thought the festivities were just about over, when the announcer returned.

"And now, the moment you've all been waiting for. That's right, folks. It's time for the traditional Victory Kiss!"

Lori had no idea what he meant. But her intuition screamed, "Trouble!" Horrified, she watched as one by one, the players' girlfriends were called out to give their guys a public good-luck smooch. Her first urge was to run back to her car, but terror had taken over her body, and her feet were rooted in place.

She was frantic. *How can I get out of this!* she asked herself hysterically. Then *her* name was called too. *If I go out there and kiss Nick, I'll be found out for sure!*

"Come on, Lori! Everyone's waiting for you!" Danielle gave Lori a hefty push, propelling her into the light.

Lori took a deep breath, gathered her courage, and ran over to Nick. The warmth in his eyes made Lori forget all about Gina Nichols. She did feel proud to be Nick's girlfriend. For a moment, she even forgot that they were kissing in front of an entire school.

"I'm glad you're here, Lori," Nick whispered in her ear just before they broke apart. "None of this would have meant anything to me without you."

Lori didn't know what to say. She just looked up at him, smiled, and blinked back her tears. "I wouldn't have missed it for anything," she said finally. Then the flash from a camera went off just a few inches from her nose. Lori blinked as spots continued to swim before her eyes. She tried to catch sight of the photographer, but he had already disappeared into the shadows.

"Who was that taking our picture, Nick? Did you notice?"

Nick shrugged. "Somebody's always taking pictures of the team. Don't worry about it, Lori. I don't think there are any reporters from *People* magazine here tonight," he said, teasing her.

A cheerleader, standing beside Nick, had over-heard their conversation. "He was from the Merivale *Mirror*. I hope he takes my picture too." The girl ran her hand through her long dark hair and pouted prettily.

I'll die if he uses my picture! Lori thought. *Or Gina Nichols will make me wish I had . . .*

As the pep rally drew to a close, the Cougars and their girlfriends decided to meet at O'Burgers, a restaurant in the mall. Shoving down her fear of being spotted with the Atwood group, Lori told Nick she'd love to go out with him and his friends.

Lori and Nick took separate cars and met in the mall lot. They were among the last to join the large group in the restaurant. When they walked in, Nick's teammates waved and called to him from a big table at the back.

"Hey—our star quarterback is here!" one of his friends shouted. "Now the party can begin!"

Lori and Nick sat down and ordered ham-burgers and Cokes. While Nick discussed foot-ball strategy with his teammates, Lori talked with their girlfriends.

"There's no way the Vikings can beat us," a girl named Caroline was saying. "I mean, Merivale hasn't beaten Atwood in twenty years."

"Merivale has a really lame team all right. The Cougars will cream them totally," another girl, Tina, agreed. "The entire school is a bunch of nerds. Did you ever see the way some of those girls dress?" she asked, making a face.

Lori hated to hear her school being put down, but she knew if she spoke up in defense of Merivale she'd cause trouble for Nick.

Pretty soon the topic of conversation turned to clothes and the latest styles. Although her taste far exceeded her budget, Lori knew loads about fashion. The Atwood girls were impressed with her comments about the latest trends from Paris and Milan.

"You're Nick's girlfriend, right?" Caroline asked Lori.

Lori nodded. "Right."

"Where do you go to school? Westwood?" Tina asked in a friendly tone.

Lori shook her head. "I go to Merivale," she said evenly. She watched the expressions on the other girls' faces. Tina, who had made the most cutting remarks about Merivale, looked embarrassed. Caroline looked shocked. Two other girls sitting nearby suddenly lost their friendly smiles and gave her a cold, hard stare that clearly said Lori was the enemy.

"Oh," Tina replied finally. "I didn't know you went there."

"Well, now you do," Lori said.

"Maybe you could have told us," Caroline said archly.

"Maybe you could have asked," Lori replied.

A chilly silence descended on the group of

girls. Before any of them could think of anything else to say, Nick turned to Lori and showed her his watch. "Look at the time. We'd better go."

"It is getting late," Lori agreed. She stood up and grabbed her purse, eager to make a fast getaway. "Good night, everybody," she said, taking Nick's hand.

"Good night," Nick's friends called back.

"See you at the big game, Lori," Tina called out. "You can sit with us. We'll save you a place. Right, girls?" she asked the others.

"Oh, for sure," Caroline chimed in. "Don't forget to look for us, Lori."

"Uh—sure," Lori said, detecting the subtly sarcastic note in their invitation.

Nick didn't notice it however. "Sounds like you girls were having a good time. What were you talking about?" he asked her as they walked toward the parking lot.

"Oh—clothes, stuff like that," Lori said with a shrug. Nick was in such a good mood that night, she didn't want to spoil it by telling him how his friends' girlfriends had reacted to her. What did it matter anyway? She had handled the situation fine without bringing Nick into it.

When they reached her car, he turned to her and drew her close. She lifted her face up to his, and they shared a long, deep kiss. "Thanks for coming to the rally tonight, Lori. It really meant a lot to me."

"You don't have to thank me, Nick. I wanted to be there," Lori whispered back.

He smiled at her, his fingertips brushing back a strand of her hair. "I know—that's why you're so special. You looked so beautiful tonight that I wouldn't be surprised if your picture was chosen to be in the paper on Monday."

"Oh, I hope not," Lori said.

When Nick laughed and kissed her again, all of Lori's worries were forgotten. She wondered how she could ever think that anything as silly as a football game could come between Nick and her.

CHAPTER FIVE

"Then what happened?" Ann asked, her slate gray eyes wide with interest. "I'll bet everyone cheered for Nick the most."

"Did you really go out and kiss him in front of all those people?" Patsy chomped down on a carrot stick and shook her head. "That took guts."

Lori shrugged. "It wasn't so bad—that is, after Danielle shoved me out there." She smiled gently, and her whole face glowed. "It *was* nice to stand next to Nick and hear everyone applauding for him and his team. He was so happy I was there."

The girls were talking in low voices, even though the Merivale High cafeteria was, as usual, a total zoo. But Patsy and Ann both knew that Lori's presence at the Atwood pep rally had to remain a closely guarded secret.

"There she is!" Patsy, Ann, and Lori looked up to see Gina Nichols marching toward them, followed by a group of cheerleaders and some guys from the Merivale football team.

Lori's heart pounded in her chest. Gina was holding up a copy of the Merivale *Mirror* and waving it above her head like a sword. Lori didn't need to read the headlines to guess what had gotten Gina so fired up.

The group circled their table, and Lori suddenly knew exactly how the pioneers in the Old West felt when their wagons were surrounded by Indians.

With a dramatic flourish, Gina tossed the newspaper onto the table, right on top of Lori's sandwich. There, on the special Monday high school sports page, for the whole world to see, was a huge photo of Lori and Nick embracing at the Atwood pep rally. "Cougar Hero Gets Victory Kiss!" the bold-type caption read.

"I was right, Randall! You are a traitor," Gina sneered. "You even went to the Atwood pep rally Friday night! No one who's anyone in this school will ever speak to you again."

"Oh, go away, Gina," Patsy shouted back. "Go try to scare someone else with your stupid threats."

Lori looked at Gina's stony face. "It's true. I was at Atwood Friday night. But I did it because my boyfriend asked me to be there." But as Lori spoke she realized that the more she said, the deeper in trouble she got.

"Oh, isn't that touching—" Gina said with mock sympathy. "I understand. My boyfriend needs me too. And we *both* want *your* support."

"Little Nicky Hobart needed her there," another Merivale cheerleader chimed in. "How sweet!"

The kids standing around Lori's lunch table murmured among themselves. Lori had the feeling that some of the kids understood her position. But Gina and her friends just wouldn't let her off the hook. They were like a pack of bloodhounds that had finally cornered its prey. *They'll stand here howling all day, if I let them*, Lori realized.

"Listen," Lori began again. "Merivale High is my school, not Atwood. My heart might be with Nick Hobart. But my loyalty is with Merivale *all* the way. And if you don't believe me—well, I don't know what else to say."

"Very pretty speech, Randall," Gina said back like a shot. "But I say actions speak louder than words. If you're really on our side, then you'll ride over to Atwood with us this afternoon. We're going to make a friendly little raid to remind them who's going to win this weekend."

"Yeah, Lori," someone in the crowd shouted. "If you're really for Merivale, you can prove it this afternoon."

Patsy and Ann gave Lori sympathetic glances. Everyone knew that the "friendly" visit to Atwood would be a wild caravan of cars flying through enemy territory. Kids would be honking horns, shouting slogans, and bombarding the opposition with shaving cream and eggs.

But when Lori glanced at the grim faces that surrounded her, she knew that if she didn't join the raid on Atwood, she might as well leave town.

"Okay," she said finally. "If that's the only way I can prove it to you all, I'll go."

After school Lori went out to the parking lot and decorated her little red Spitfire with crepe paper, balloons, and a big sign that read, "Crush Atwood!" Patsy and Ann helped, of course. They wouldn't make Lori go through with it alone, so they were riding with her.

"Well, looks like the car should pass Gina's inspection," Lori said to her friends. "But what about Nick? He's going to recognize it—to say nothing of me. Do you think I should hold a sign in front of my face while I'm driving? Of course, I might drive into a tree or something. . . ."

"I've got a better idea," Patsy said. "The drama club has a big trunkful of costumes and masks. I'll just borrow a few for us. Nick doesn't have to know that you were in the raid. He could think someone borrowed your car."

"Great idea, Patsy!" Lori wasn't convinced, and she didn't even want to guess what Nick would say if he found out she was in on the raid. *But maybe he won't see us,* Lori thought, trying to calm herself down.

A few minutes later Gina Nichols and Jack Baxter gave the signal for the caravan to pull out. Gina was sitting next to Jack in the lead car, a big convertible that was packed with Jack's teammates and their cheerleader girlfriends.

With horns blaring, the long line of cars snaked out of the Merivale High student parking lot and headed toward Atwood. Lori maneuvered her car into the tail end position. As soon as Atwood came into sight, each girl pulled a full rubber Halloween mask over her head.

Lori was wearing a werewolf mask. It was hot inside, and she could barely see enough of the road to drive. *But as long as Nick won't recognize me, I don't care if I suffocate in here,* she thought.

The parade of cars and raucous students streamed through the gates of Atwood Academy. The Atwood students, who were just being dismissed, poured out of the buildings to see what was happening. Blasting horns heralded Merivale's arrival, and the cars careened around the school buildings and out to the athletic fields.

Groups of Atwood students chased the cars on foot. Shaving cream and egg bombs began to fly and soon the scene looked like a war zone.

With a glob of shaving cream stuck to her mask and another to one shoulder, Lori gamely followed close behind the other cars in the parade. She hadn't caught sight of Nick—she hoped he was changing for practice already.

Finally Gina gave the signal for the Merivale caravan to leave. Lori breathed a tremendous sigh of relief. The Atwood gates were already in sight. Just a few seconds and this whole stupid thing would be over, she promised herself.

But just as Lori was about to exit through the gate, a group of Nick's teammates surrounded her car. Two of them jumped on the hood.

"You big bozos!" Patsy shouted from under her mask. "Get out of here!" Pushing on one of them, Patsy and Ann finally managed to shove him away.

But now a large, angry mob had formed a human roadblock in front of Lori's car. And Lori had to slam on her brakes at the last second to keep from running them over.

"Get out of the way," Lori shouted, honking her horn and praying they would let her pass. "I'll drive right through you guys. I mean it—"

"Go ahead and try it. We dare you!" A football player dressed in his uniform reached into the car and pulled at Lori's mask. "Let's just see who's under here. I like to look the enemy right in the eye—"

Lori fought back, but he was stronger than she. He pulled the mask over her head.

"Hobart's girlfriend!" he shouted.

"I don't believe it!" another one said.

A third leaned over and took a good look at Lori. "Yeah—that's her! And I *do* believe it!"

In the confusion the human chain broke apart and Lori gunned her engine. The little car roared through the gates with the players chasing behind it on foot for a couple of minutes.

The dust had barely settled in the Atwood parking lot before the outraged, egg-smeared students began organizing a counterattack on Merivale High.

Danielle had witnessed the Merivale raid and definitely wanted to take part in Atwood's revenge plan. But she had a few things to do before she drove over to the day-care center. She really dreaded another session there. *I can't believe I'm really going back there today. I haven't fully recovered from Friday's visit.*

But just as Danielle was heading for her car, she met Teresa and Heather. *What luck! Here come the last two people in the universe I feel like talking to right now.*

"Hey, Danielle!" Heather called as they walked quickly toward her. "Where're you going?"

"Everyone's over in the quad," Teresa said, "planning our raid on Merivale. Don't you want to know what's happening?"

"Uh—sure. Listen, call me tonight and tell me all about it. I really have to run—"

"You know, if you're seeing some new guy, we'll just find out anyway." Teresa blew her brown bangs out of her eyes. "You might as well just tell us who it is now."

Danielle laughed at both of them. "What makes you think I'm sneaking off to see somebody? Why would I want to keep something like that a secret?" she asked, trying to convince them she really was seeing someone new.

Teresa—who thrived on secrets and any gossip she could dig up—persisted. "Why don't you tell us about him? Is he really weird?"

"What a genius. Of course I'm sneaking around to meet a loser," Danielle replied in a tone dripping with sarcasm. "You know how boring it can get going out with all the great guys who are always calling—" She gave Teresa a wicked smile. "Then again, maybe you *don't* know. See you—"

While Teresa tried to figure out some equally stinging comeback, Danielle swiftly walked across the parking lot and jumped into her BMW.

You're not going to weasel the truth out of me that easily, Teresa. I might have failed that psych exam— but I still know how to handle you!

Up in Lori's bedroom the girls hurriedly cleaned themselves up. They were all late for work.

"Why did I ever let Gina Nichols bully me into going on that raid?" Lori asked her friends as she pulled a comb through her long blond hair. "Nick is going to be furious when he finds out I was part of that. He'll probably never speak to me again."

"He'll understand, Lori," Ann said, assuring her. "Haven't you told him how Gina's been on your case all week about that dumb button?"

Lori shook her head. "Gina *is* a total pain, but Nick is so worried about the game that I don't want to bother him with my problems too."

"Well, maybe if you tell him the whole story, he'll understand why you did it," Patsy said.

He'll never understand how I could be so disloyal to him. Lori nervously tugged on a lock of her hair. "I hope so," was all she said out loud.

Danielle pulled into the mall parking lot and breathed a sigh of relief. *That was close—I wonder how much longer I can keep this up. I guess I can make Heather and Teresa think I'm seeing some new guy just until my fifteen hours are up. Putting up with their nosy questions is certainly a lot better than hearing them tease me about working at the day-care center for a good grade in Mrs. Ellis's class.*

Danielle parked her car in a space close to one of the mall's large, midpriced department stores. She *rarely* shopped in department stores. Unless it was one of the famous stores on Fifth Avenue in New York where her mother sometimes took her as a special treat. Most of her beautiful clothes were purchased at elegant boutiques like Facades. But Danielle knew that she would never find the outfit she needed at Facades.

About fifteen minutes later Danielle walked out of the store with her purchase. She cringed. If anyone ever saw her wearing the outfit she had just bought . . . But nobody except the kids at the center and Betsy Harper would.

The shopping bag contained a plain blue sweat suit, which she planned to change into as soon as she got to the center. It was bad enough that she had to spend fifteen whole hours with that pack of screaming, crying little monsters. But she didn't have to ruin her gorgeous wardrobe in the process. That would be carrying this whole thing too far!

As Danielle wove her way through the lines of cars to her own, she heard someone quietly call her name. "Danielle, Danielle." Then it stopped. *Must have been my imagination.*

"Danielle. Danielle."

What is this? Someone's playing a joke. She turned in a full three-hundred-and-sixty-degree circle. No one there. *Oh, no. Yes, there is.* Just to her left she thought she saw a dark head duck down behind the hood of that red Volvo. *Two can play this silly little game,* she thought, dropping down and moving in a duck waddle between cars until she was on the opposite side of the Volvo. She was going to get this joker!

She waited patiently, knowing that he'd have to poke his head up to see where she had gone. *Here he comes! Now!* "Surpr—" she started to yell, but stopped when she found herself looking straight into the gypsy black eyes of Don James. Slowly, the two of them rose on either side of the hood. Danielle was unable to say anything—she just stood there, never taking her eyes from his.

Neither of them smiled—they just looked. Finally Don spoke. "Hey, Red. How's it going?" This he said in a measured, soft drawl, and the right corner of his mouth slowly picked up in a lazy grin. The smile quickly reached his eyes and lit up his craggy, handsome face.

"Hi," was all she managed to get out. Why did he always affect her like this? She had to look away to break his hold on her. Forcing her eyes back, she said, "How's *what* going?"

"I don't know. Had any good pizza lately?" he asked, his grin still in place. They both knew he was referring to the night they had gone out for pizza with Lori and Nick.

Whenever she thought of that night or of Don James, she developed the heady, exhilarated feeling of someone driving too fast—or of someone in love. But that she knew was impossible, even though he was the handsomest boy she had ever seen.

Nice girls didn't talk to Don James, much less go out with him. He had a reputation as being wild and a born troublemaker. After he graduated from Merivale High, he wanted to be an auto mechanic in town. Danielle Sharp, with an auto mechanic for a boyfriend! No, she just couldn't let it happen to her, no matter how he made her heart dance.

He moved slowly around the front of the car and stood looking down at her. The sun, low in the afternoon sky, framed his head like a halo. And Danielle didn't know what hurt more to look at, the sun or his wonderful face.

A dog yipped and reached a paw out to brush against her skirt. For the first time Danielle looked down and noticed the large, golden, mixed-breed dog at Don's side. Happy for the diversion, Danielle bent down to pat the dog's silky head.

"Hi, Garbo," she said, greeting the dog she had found as a stray and given to Don.

"So what do you say? Want to join me and Garbo for a walk by the lake?" Don asked.

"I wish," Danielle said and blushed at the honesty of her answer. She quickly explained her predicament with Mrs. Ellis's psych class and the day-care center. "I'm due over there in about ten minutes," Danielle said. "Betsy asked me to think up some activities to keep the kids busy this afternoon. And I don't know what to do. You should see them, they're terribly wild."

"Sounds like my kind of group," Don said, joking. "Where did you say this place was?"

"Don—I'm not kidding. How am I ever going to keep those kids entertained?"

Just then, as if on cue, Garbo lay down at Danielle's feet. She rolled on her back and whimpered, her signal that she wanted her stomach scratched.

Don and Danielle looked at each other, both having the same idea at once. "I've got it! Can I take Garbo with me? She's bound to distract the kids for a while," Danielle said.

"This dog loves a party," Don said. "She'll keep those kids entertained for hours."

"Hey, you silly hound, want to come with me to the day-care center?" Danielle asked the dog. Garbo sat up and barked. Don and Danielle looked at each other and laughed.

"Well, I guess you found yourself a volunteer," Don said. He agreed to pick up Garbo at the center later.

"Well, see you—" Danielle said, not really wanting to leave. She picked up the dog's leash. "I have a feeling this just might work out."

"What might work out?" Don asked.

"The dog," she said, smiling in spite of herself. "Well, it sure was great luck meeting you this way, Don."

Don gave her one of his famous slow grins. "Hey, ladies who meet up with me are always lucky, Red. I've been trying to tell you that all along. See you girls later."

Although Danielle had dreaded her afternoon at the center, her second day went smoother than the first. Garbo was a great hit with the children and provided a perfect distraction for them. Danielle let Garbo loose on the playground outside, and the dog romped with the children tirelessly.

After their workout with Garbo, the kids were exhausted. They trooped back inside, and Danielle read them a story. *Funny*, she thought. The children were no longer a sea of crying, whining faces—now she knew most of them by name. She was even learning their various likes and dislikes.

Soon the children's parents arrived to pick them up. And Danielle was almost sorry to see the kids go!

"I'm so glad you've started working here, Danielle," Betsy said as they were straightening up the playroom. "Bringing your dog was a stroke of genius."

"Just a lucky guess, actually," Danielle replied. *Or fate*, she added silently.

Don James always seemed to be there when

she needed help. Maybe fate was trying to tell her something. Maybe—

Don't be ridiculous, Danielle, she chided herself. *You know it's impossible. He's all wrong for you.*

Still, when she heard Don's footsteps on the porch outside the day-care center, Danielle couldn't stop her heart from pounding. He was here! And no matter what her logical side kept telling her, her heart was saying *I can't wait to see him.*

CHAPTER SIX

"Lori—I can't believe you!" Nick's aquamarine eyes flashed with anger. Lori wished that the ground would open up and swallow her. But she knew that she wasn't going to have any such luck.

They were standing outside Tio's. Lori had just finished work and found him waiting outside for her. "I guess you heard I was at Atwood today—" Lori began in a faltering voice.

"It should have been on the six o'clock news! Every single guy on the team told me. You made me look like a jerk!"

"Wait, Nick, you don't understand. It didn't have anything to do with you—"

"You're right. I *don't* understand. The way I see it, it had everything to do with me."

"Nick! Please don't say that! I care about you more than anything!" In another second Lori was going to burst into tears. The situation was becoming absolutely hopeless.

"Well, you sure have a crazy way of showing it!"

Lori sighed. "Listen, can't we please go someplace quiet and talk this over?" *If I'm going to break up with Nick tonight, at least I'd like to do it in private*, she thought grimly.

"All right. We'll go over to O'Burgers," Nick said. "And get a table in the back."

Once seated, Lori tried to explain how Gina Nichols had been following her around like a private detective, trying to prove that Lori had no school spirit and was a traitor to Merivale High. Nick gave her a sympathetic look and reached across the table to take her hand.

"Then Gina found that stupid picture in the newspaper this morning, and the entire school thought I was a traitor. If I didn't join in on the raid at Atwood, I don't think I could ever show up at Merivale High again."

At the mention of the raid on his school, Nick's expression darkened again, and he let go of her hand. "Give me a break, Lori, you *didn't* have to come to Atwood if you didn't really want to—"

Lori began to get angry. He wasn't even trying to see her side of it. "Nick! You're not even listening to me! I know it's hard for you. But it's hard for me too. I'm caught in the middle."

"Yeah, well, at least you don't have to go to

practice, wondering where your girlfriend is going to turn up next," he said harshly. "One of the guys even joked that maybe I was planning to throw the game in your honor."

"Nick! He can't honestly think you'd try to lose the game. What an awful thing to say—"

"Yeah, but I have a gut feeling he was serious about it," Nick added, staring off over Lori's head. His expression was stony.

Lori didn't know what to say. Nick was losing the confidence of his teammates because of her. But darn it! She had a lot of pressure on her as well. Couldn't he understand that? If only he'd try to see what she was going through. "I can't believe things are getting so screwed up between us because of this dumb school rivalry," Lori said glumly.

Nick sighed. "Yeah—well, maybe it's more important than you think, Lori."

Lori was alarmed by his serious tone. "What does that mean?"

Nick shrugged. "I don't know—whatever you think it means." He fiddled with the straw in his soda and finally crushed it in his hand. With a sad look on his face, he shook his head. "I think we've talked enough—I'm going home."

He stood up and started to snap his Cougar jacket. Lori was stunned. He was really going to leave.

"Nick, wait. I want you to win, you know that. It's just that I'm so, well, confused—"

"Lori," Nick said. "You just said it. You're confused. When you get *unconfused*, give me a call."

Dumbfounded, Lori watched as Nick paid their bill and left the restaurant. Her eyes welled up with tears, and she hoped no one was watching.

Maybe if she just let him think things over, he'd see that she was being forced to make an impossible choice!

On Wednesday Danielle had agreed to meet Teresa and Heather at the mall's six-plex movie theater. Danielle had successfully avoided them for the past couple of days. But they were really demanding to see her. And Danielle thought if they went to the movies, there wouldn't be much opportunity for them to interrogate her about her after-school activities.

"Let's go over to Video Arcade," Heather suggested.

"And see who's hanging out," Danielle added.

"Good idea," Teresa agreed. She took a compact out of her purse and checked her hair as they walked along. *Go ahead and primp, Teresa,* Danielle thought and snickered to herself. No matter what Teresa did to herself, Danielle knew *she* always got all the male attention. That night she was wearing a great pair of tight blue leather pants and a gorgeous white angora cowl neck sweater. Not a single teenage male had passed her by without sending her a glance.

"Are we looking for anyone in particular, Danielle?" Heather asked.

"Yeah, maybe the mystery man that you've been running off to meet every day after school," Teresa suggested. "Why didn't you see him tonight—instead of us?"

Danielle just smiled. Sometimes, Teresa and Heather were even more gullible than the little kids at the day-care center. Danielle could see now that it wasn't going to be any problem to string them along for another few days.

"It's only a quarter to nine," Danielle replied with a sly smile. She looked down at her beautifully manicured nails and ran her fingers through her hair. "Maybe I am going to see him—after I'm finished with you two."

"I knew it," Teresa said. "I was wondering why you were so dressed up, just for a movie."

"Come on, Danielle. *Please* tell us who it is," Heather begged. "I promise we won't tell a soul, will we, Teresa?"

"My lips are sealed," Teresa solemnly vowed.

Danielle wanted to laugh out loud. Telling Heather or Teresa a secret was like having the news plastered on a billboard.

"Now, now, ladies. I never said I was *definitely* seeing anybody," Danielle said, taunting them.

"Let's skip the arcade and go over to The Big Scoop," Teresa suggested. "A lot of cute guys hang out there. Maybe a little hot fudge will loosen your tongue, Danielle."

"Maybe," Danielle said, feeling as if she were a cat playing with two silly mice. "And then again, maybe not."

CHAPTER SEVEN

The next two days passed slowly for Lori. Every night she rushed home from work, hoping there would be a message for her from Nick. But each night, her spirits took a crash dive when she learned he hadn't called. Since he was busy with football practice, there wasn't even any chance for her to run into him at the mall. She wanted to call him . . . but she was afraid. What if he was still mad at her? Or worse yet, what if he thought they'd really broken up at O'Burgers?

On Wednesday evening she was helping her mother clean up the kitchen when the phone rang. Lori got so nervous, she dropped a plate.

"What a klutz I am," Lori mumbled as she stared down at the broken bits of china. It was the third dish she had broken that week! With a sigh, she bent over and began picking up the pieces.

Staring curiously at her daughter, Cynthia Randall walked over and answered the ringing phone. Lori held her breath as she waited to see who was calling. When she heard that the call was for her eleven-year-old brother Teddy, she felt a sudden tightness in her chest, as if she were about to cry. She dropped the pieces of the plate. Then she started to sob.

"Lori—" Her mother walked over and put her arm around Lori's shoulders. "Never mind about the plate. What's the real reason you're crying? Anything you want to talk about?"

Lori shrugged and wiped her tears away with the back of her hand. "Me? I'm fine—honest."

Her mother stood and looked at her and waited. "Come on, honey. You've been as jumpy as a cat. How's Nick?"

That was her mom—she had a knack for understanding and getting right to the heart of the matter. It was all her years of working as a nurse and listening to people's problems. Lori and she sat down at the kitchen table.

"Uh—I don't know how Nick is. We sort of had a fight, and I haven't heard from him in a couple of days."

"This sounds serious. What did you fight about?"

Lori shrugged. "Something really stupid."

"Most arguments are over something stupid. But you want to know something? I'll bet Nick is moping around his house, just as you are.

He's probably afraid to call because he thinks *you're* still mad at *him*. Why don't you call him?"

"You really think I should?" Lori asked her mother hopefully.

Her mother smiled and began loading the rest of the dishes into the dishwasher. "It's worth a try. Besides, if someone doesn't make the first move soon, this family will have to eat off paper plates."

Lori took a deep breath, straightened her shoulders, and said, "Okay, I'll give him a call."

A short time later Lori went up to her room and dialed Nick's number—the number that was so familiar to her. But that night she dialed it with a sense of dread. She was terribly nervous and her voice was shaking when she said hello. But Nick sounded so happy to hear from her, Lori soon realized her mother had given her good advice.

They talked about school and work for a while, then Nick brought up the topic they were both afraid to mention. "I'm sorry we had a fight the other day, Lori. I've been feeling just awful about the whole mess—"

"I feel terrible too," Lori confessed. "I was afraid to call you. I thought when you left O'Burgers the other night—well, I thought that you were breaking up with me."

"Breaking up with you? I was mad, but I don't want to break up! Listen, let's not even talk about the game or any of that stuff, okay? Maybe I don't understand your feelings, but that doesn't mean I want us to split."

The last couple of days of gloom were suddenly forgotten and Lori felt her spirits soar again. "Okay, it's a deal. We won't say another word about it."

"It's not *exactly* what I want," Nick admitted honestly. "But I guess it'll have to do for now."

Lori could tell he was still upset with her. *But at least he doesn't want to break up. Maybe things will work out all right after all. . . .*

"Wow—you really called him? That took guts," Ann said to Lori that next morning as they drove to school. "I rarely call Ron. Of course I do see him constantly. Except this last week because of his paper."

She was referring to Ron Taylor, the college freshman she was dating. They both worked at the Body Shoppe.

"It was worse wondering if Nick had broken up with me," Lori admitted. "He said he still didn't really understand my problem. But we both promised not to fight about it anymore."

Ann looked happy to hear the good news. "You and Nick are the perfect couple, Lori," she said. "No way you guys are going to break up over a silly thing like a football game!"

"I'm glad *someone* around here is so sure about that," Lori said with a laugh.

"Come on, Lori—Saturday is the big game. Before you know it, your troubles will be over and everything'll be back to normal."

Lori pulled her car into a space in the Merivale High student parking lot. "I just wish I could blink my eyes and it would be Sunday," Lori confessed. "I'm afraid of what might happen next. This whole football thing is turning my life into a bad dream."

"Speaking of bad dreams," Ann whispered, "here comes Gina Nichols."

"Oh, no! Not the first thing in the morning," Lori whispered back. "I don't know how much more of this I can take."

As the girls got out of Lori's car, Gina boldly strolled up to them.

"Where's your button, Randall?" Gina asked, inspecting Lori's outfit as if she were a drill sergeant.

"Hi, Gina. Nice to see you too." Lori flashed the nasty cheerleader a dazzling smile.

Ann stepped next to Lori and gave her a quick nudge with her elbow. What was Lori trying to do? If she kept this up, she'd be on Gina's hit list again in no time!

Ann could see that Gina really meant business this time. But Lori just crossed her arms and met Gina's intimidating gaze with an icy blue stare of her own.

"Here, Lori—" Ann pulled off her own button and started to pin it on Lori's sweater. "Why don't you wear mine? I think I have an extra in my locker."

"No thanks." Lori smiled briefly at her friend as she refused the offer. "I'm not wearing a button today, Gina, because I just don't feel like it. And if you don't like it, that's tough."

Gina looked shocked for an instant, then her face turned red. "Oh, it's going to be tough, all right—tough on you. You didn't fool me for a second, Randall. I knew you weren't on *our* side, even though you did a good job *pretending* to be."

"I wasn't pretending, Gina. I have as much school loyalty as anyone else around here. But I'm sick and tired of you trying to push me around!" Other kids were starting to stop and listen, but Lori didn't care. *I should have told Gina off long ago, instead of letting her bully me.*

"But your boyfriend at Atwood—" Gina began.

"You leave Nick out of this! You're all expecting me to make an impossible choice. I refuse to have any part of this stupid school rivalry for another minute. From now on," Lori declared, "consider me a totally *neutral* bystander. Come on, Ann." Lori glanced at her friend, who had grown rather pale. "We're going to be late for class."

"Right." Ann hurried after Lori, glancing back a few times at the dumbfounded Gina.

"Well, you sure told her off," Ann said, congratulating Lori as they went into the building. "She didn't have a thing to say."

"Don't worry," Lori replied with a weak smile. "I'm sure it won't take her long to recover."

That afternoon at Atwood everyone was getting ready for the sneak raid on Merivale High. Cars were decorated with streamers and big signs. Cans of shaving cream and eggs were stockpiled in the parking lot, ready for an all-out attack.

Danielle got into her car to go to the day-care center. *It's a lucky break that Heather and Teresa have the raid—they won't be able to question me today.*

Humming a favorite song, Danielle cruised out of the Atwood parking lot. In a couple of days the day-care center would be history, and her life would be back to normal. *I'll have to hint around to Teresa and Heather that my "hot romance" sizzled out. I do like working with the kids,* she admitted to herself. *But I also miss hanging out. All work and no play is just not my style.*

As she cruised along the wide, tree-lined avenues of Merivale, Danielle was preoccupied, thinking of Don James and how different he was from her friends. Look at the way he dressed. He was always in Levis and a worn leather jacket. *Definitely not a preppy. But most definitely gorgeous.*

She was so lost in thought that she didn't

even notice Teresa's silver Corvette just a few cars behind hers.

"Don't get too close," Heather said to Teresa. "We don't want her to spot us!"

"Don't worry." Still keeping the white BMW in sight, Teresa steered her car into the slow lane. "If she didn't notice us by now, she's not going to. Besides, she thinks we went on the Merivale raid. Danielle wouldn't suspect she was being followed today—not in a million years."

"I hate to miss trashing Merivale," Heather replied. "But catching Danielle red-handed with her new boy is loads more fun, don't you think?"

"For sure," Teresa agreed emphatically.

"I thought she'd tell us who he is by now," Heather said. "Well, we gave her a chance to come clean."

"I think we've been *too* nice about it. It's time Danielle got a taste of her own medicine," Teresa said vindictively. "If this guy was a hunk, she'd let everyone in town know about him, believe me. He's probably a real creep."

"Probably," Heather agreed.

"Look! She's pulling up to that yellow building. She must be meeting him someplace around here."

Danielle found a parking spot directly in front of the day-care center. She took her sweat suit out of her car and went inside. Teresa parked her car a short distance down the block.

"Come on, Heather. She went in there. The sign says it's a day-care center—maybe he's a teacher!"

"An older man! That really would be something."

The girls hurried across the street and—as unobtrusively as possible—tried to peer into the windows. But before they could move, Danielle suddenly appeared, in a sweat suit, following a pack of kids outside. The children ran screaming into the playground.

"Teresa! Heather!" Danielle was shocked at the sight of her friends. How in the world had they found her? What could she possibly tell them now? "What are *you* doing here?"

"That's funny," Teresa said. "We were about to ask you the same thing."

"So—where's your mystery man, Danielle?" Heather asked her. "Or maybe there never was a guy, after all—just a herd of noisy little kids. Isn't that a laugh!"

"And check out that sweat suit!" Teresa pointed to Danielle's inexpensive jogging outfit. "Oh, my! Where did you pick that up? Monsieur K-mart?"

"I can't believe you followed me," Danielle replied, her green eyes glowing dangerously.

"And we can't believe that you've been sneaking off for baby-sitting duty!" Teresa was plainly delighted that her detective work had paid off so handsomely. "What's the matter, Danielle? Mommy and Daddy take away your allowance?"

Although Danielle's family was quite rich, Teresa and Heather's parents were even wealthier. The two girls never failed to hold it over Danielle.

"I don't get a cent for doing this, for your information, Teresa," Danielle snapped. "It's volunteer work. I do it because I like it."

"Oh, how very noble of you, Danielle," Teresa crooned. "Why, I think I even see a halo glowing around her head. Do you see it too, Heather?"

"Definitely," Heather agreed, taking part in the joke. "I think little wings have sprouted on her back too. She's just too, too *wonderful* for words."

"You two are really pathetic!" Danielle laughed. She wanted to tell them why she was really working at the center. But she had already gotten herself in too deep, playing the role of the dedicated volunteer.

"Why should I even bother to explain why I come here to you?" Danielle said haughtily. With a light shrug of her shoulders, she turned and followed the children into the playground. "I've got work to do. See you around. . . ."

News spread quickly that day of Lori's "declaration of independence." Gina was still trying to smear her, telling everyone that Lori was pro-Atwood.

Lori noticed that quite a few kids did snub

her because of Gina's influence. But she didn't care. If they were so quick to believe Gina's slander, it meant that they weren't real friends anyway. Of course, Patsy and Ann stuck by her. Lori knew that no matter what, they always would.

After school the three of them went over to the mall to buy a pair of black jeans for Ann before they went to work. They jammed into a dressing room at Pants Patio, while Ann tried on a pile of jeans and a bunch of tops that had caught her eye.

"I would have given anything to have been there this morning and watched you tell Gina off," Patsy said. She was sitting on a stool with a heap of clothes in her lap.

"Lori was hot all right." Ann yanked up the zipper on a pair of jeans and checked her reflection in the mirror. "I guess since you and Nick made up, you want him to know you're on his side. Anybody could understand that, Lori. After all, he is your boyfriend."

Lori sighed and shook her head. Even her *best* friends didn't understand. "I told Gina that from now on, I wasn't taking sides and I meant it. It's the only fair way. I just can't make a choice. I feel loyalty for Merivale—and Nick too. But I won't be bounced back and forth like a Ping-Pong ball anymore. The kids at school will have to accept it—and so will Nick."

*　　*　　*

Trying her best to ignore Heather and Teresa, Danielle began organizing a game with the kids. They played Farmer in the Dell and London Bridge. Then they stopped for a cookie and milk break before playing again.

The kids then asked to play a game called Bluebird. Danielle didn't know it, but it was fun to have the children teach her for a change. They made a big circle, held hands, and then sang a special song while one child, the bluebird, walked around the outside of the circle and picked other kids to join him. Soon there was a whole line of kids, weaving their way in and out of the circle and singing the song in their sweet little voices.

Danielle was having so much fun, she didn't even notice Heather and Teresa watching her with the children.

"Come on, Heather. Let's get out of here. I'm going to die from a sugar overdose if I watch any more of this."

Heather, however, couldn't seem to pull herself away. "I don't know. I just don't get it. Something fishy is going on here. Why would Danielle—of *all* people—be doing this?"

Teresa glanced at Danielle. "Yeah, you're right. The whole thing is kind of strange."

"She's pulling something over on us. I just know it," Heather said. "Let's tell her we want to volunteer, too, and see what she says. Maybe we'll find out what's going on."

"Good idea!" Teresa said gleefully.

It was time to take the kids back inside, and Danielle rounded up the rowdy bunch and did a quick head count as they passed through the playground gate.

Heather and Teresa were waiting to speak to her again at the doorway. "Hey, Danielle, you really looked like you were having fun out there," Teresa said with a hesitant smile.

"You get along with the kids so well," Heather added with real admiration in her voice. "They *really* listen to you."

"They're just average, energy-packed pre-schoolers." Danielle shrugged. Her friends had certainly changed. But was it another trick?

"Well, I guess you have to go inside now." Teresa looked down, avoiding Danielle's curious stare. "Listen, I'm sorry for what I said before—teasing you about being here and all."

"I am too, Danielle," Heather chimed in. "I'm really impressed that you're volunteering your time like this. Do you think we could do it too?"

"Maybe Heather and I could both help out here with you. Wouldn't that be fun?" Teresa asked.

Danielle didn't know what to say. How had she gotten herself into another predicament? If Heather and Teresa started working there, they'd certainly find out the truth—that she wasn't volunteering out of the goodness of her heart, but doing it for a better grade in Mrs. Ellis's class. There had to be some way out of this—

"Well, it's really nice of you both to offer. But I don't think the center needs any more volunteers right now."

Heather and Teresa looked very disappointed. "Maybe we should go inside and ask for ourselves," Heather suggested, glancing at Teresa.

"Uh—no, don't do that," Danielle said, quickly interrupting. She had a feeling Betsy Harper would give the whole thing away if Heather and Teresa got to speak with her. "I've got a great idea! I'm taking the kids on a special trip to the mall, next Monday after school. Why don't you two meet me there and help with supervising them?"

Teresa and Heather looked at each other. Finally Teresa spoke up for both of them. "Sure— that sounds like fun. We'd love to help you, wouldn't we, Heather?"

"Sounds like fun to me," Heather agreed with another smile. "I don't know why you made such a big secret of this, Danielle."

Danielle couldn't believe how her super-aloof friends were getting into this field trip idea. *It really will be fun to have Heather and Teresa along,* she thought. *And this way Betsy won't have to go. The three of us can easily handle them.*

Danielle led the children back inside as her friends walked toward Teresa's car. Inside the car Heather and Teresa collapsed against each other, laughing. "That was great!" Teresa said. "She *really* thinks we want to help out with that pack of brats."

"Did you see the look on her face when we said we'd help her? Anybody with the intelligence of a houseplant should know that we'd rather be dead than seen hanging out in the mall with a bunch of screaming babies."

Catching her breath from laughing, Teresa checked her reflection in the rearview mirror. "Just wait until we don't show up and she has to handle those kids all alone."

"It's going to be great all right." Teresa started up the car and pulled away from the curb. "I don't know what Danielle is up to, but this should teach her not to try to trick us."

"I can hardly wait to give her the good news," Teresa smirked in agreement.

CHAPTER EIGHT

Lori, Ann, and Patsy were practically the only kids who didn't take part in the battle scene at Merivale High. They were all at work.

The rest of the Merivale students, however, had heard about the Atwood raid and were ready for it. Armed with the usual ammunition of shaving cream and eggs, they ran out of the school buildings and surrounded the Atwood caravan. The school grounds looked like a disaster area, as did the Atwood cars, when the battle was over.

When Nick called Lori the night before, neither of them had even mentioned the raid. They talked about anything and everything *but* the Atwood-Merivale rivalry. But, Lori told herself, in two days it would be over. She just had to endure until the game on Saturday.

"I feel like I'm hiding out from the police or something," Lori complained to Ann and Patsy on Friday. "Thank heavens this is going to be over tomorrow. I couldn't hold out any longer, I'm ready to crack up."

The three girls were driving to their jobs at the mall after school. "The game *is* tomorrow. If you can just hang in, Lori, you'll be home free," Patsy said encouragingly.

"Yeah, Lor. You've done a good job staying out of the line of fire so far. Nick isn't mad at you anymore and even Gina has gotten off your case," Ann said. "What can possibly happen between now and tomorrow to foul things up?"

Lori frowned as she searched for a parking spot. She couldn't put it into words. It was just a funny feeling.

"I don't know, guys. I just have this feeling that it's not over yet."

Her friends reassured her that she was worrying needlessly, and Lori felt a little better. But then she glanced at her parking space number. All the good feelings were instantly replaced by a sudden chill. *Out of all the spaces in the entire lot, I had to pick number thirteen!* Lori couldn't help but feel it was an omen of things to come. . . .

At Tio's, business was brisk. Lori was stationed at the register behind the counter taking orders. She didn't mind the fast pace; it took her mind off her worries and made the time pass quickly. When the crowd of customers finally dwindled, she glanced at the clock and was amazed to see that she had only an hour or so left before she could go home.

See, silly, you were only being superstitious. Nothing bad is going to happen. . . .

But only seconds later Lori heard Gina Nichols's voice. She quickly glanced up to see Gina and a large group of the Merivale Vikings piling into Tio's.

Oh, darn! Gina and her friends were the last people on earth Lori wanted to deal with right then. *Maybe I can trade places with someone in the kitchen for a while!*

Lori quickly left the counter and stepped through the big swinging doors marked Employees Only. But, just as her luck would have it, she walked smack into her boss, Ernie Goldbloom.

Ernie gave her a puzzled look. "What are you doing back here? I thought I stationed you behind the counter."

"I—uh, just thought someone might want to switch with me for a while. It got kind of slow out there."

"Slow? With that gang of kids that just walked in?" Ernie gently took hold of Lori's shoulders and turned her around. "To your register, Lori. They look hungry to me."

Lori had no choice. Taking a deep breath, she pushed through the swinging doors and headed back to the counter. She readied herself for another showdown with Gina. *Just remember,* she told herself, *you are neutral. Neutral, neutral, neutral—Nick!*

Lori was amazed to see Nick standing there instead of Gina. "Wh-what are you doing here?"

Nick laughed. "Looking for you, of course. Where have you been?"

"I—uh—had to go in the kitchen for a minute." Lori quickly glanced around, looking for Gina and the group of Merivale Vikings. They were sitting at a corner table, and she guessed that Nick hadn't noticed them yet. "Are you alone?"

"Nope. A bunch of guys from the team are meeting me here. I told you we'd stop by after practice today. What's the matter? You don't seem very happy to see me—"

A *bunch* of Atwood Cougars! Lori felt as if Nick had just told her that he brought along a case of dynamite.

"Of course I'm happy to see you—" Lori glanced across the room at Gina's table eyeing them. "But take a look over there. Maybe you and your friends should eat someplace else," Lori gently suggested.

Nick followed her gaze and when he turned back his jaw was set. "We have as much right to hang out here as *they* do. Just let them try anything—"

The look of determination in Nick's blue eyes made Lori suddenly afraid of what might happen.

"Oh, Nick, please don't get into a fight. The

game is tomorrow. What if you got hurt and couldn't play? You don't want that to happen," Lori said quickly, trying to appeal to his rational side.

But when it came to the Vikings, it was clear that Nick didn't think rationally.

"You know me. I'd never look for trouble. But if there's a fight, believe me, the Cougars aren't going to be the ones to get hurt."

Before Lori could even reply, shouts were heard as the rest of the Cougars sauntered in and the two teams caught sight of each other.

"Hey, Cougars, we were here first!" a brawny Merivale linebacker yelled. "Just haul it out of here—if you don't want to get hurt."

"Oh, yeah?" one of Nick's teammates shouted back. "Tough guy. Want to try to *make* us?" Lori cringed, terrified of what would happen next.

"Well, I think you guys had better get out and go home to rest up," another of Nick's friends shouted. "Tomorrow you're going to be dead meat!"

"That's a laugh!" Gina called back. "The *mighty* Cougars won't be roaring for long. Not after the Vikings get through with them!"

"That's right—we're the team that's finally going to smear you all over the field," Jack Baxter yelled. "They'll have to shovel you up and send you home in pillowcases. Ask anybody—ask

Hobart's own girlfriend," he shouted, pointing a finger at Lori.

All eyes were suddenly on Lori. She glanced around nervously, rubbing her hands on her apron. Her gaze met Nick's, and she hoped that he'd say something to help her out.

"Go ahead, Lori," Nick said, staring at her. "Tell them who's going to get smeared tomorrow—and who's going to do the *smearing*."

Lori felt her face flush. She bit down on her lip. *Why am I always caught in the middle like this? It just isn't fair*, she said to herself. Then she remembered her resolution. Speaking in as steady a voice as she could muster, she said, "The team that plays the hardest will win."

Nick stepped back, shocked. She could tell in an instant that he was furious with her answer.

"What do you mean by that?" he asked in a cold voice. "You actually do believe the Vikings are going to win, don't you?"

"I never said that," Lori replied, trying to defend herself. "I just meant that—"

"You little traitor!" Gina shouted. "If you can't just come right out and say Merivale will win, you really do belong on *their* side."

"Listen, I think *both* teams are great. I can't possibly predict which one will win."

Nick and his friends just glared at her. She could see the disappointment in Nick's eyes, and it hurt her. The group from Merivale looked just as disgruntled. They had wanted to hear

Lori voice her loyalty. Nobody wanted to hear that the two teams were equally matched.

"Yeah, we heard it all before, Randall," Gina said. "But the stadium has two sides. And tomorrow you'll have to pick one."

"Come on, guys." Jack Baxter, his black hair slicked straight back, signaled his friends and slung his arm over Gina's shoulder. "Let's blow."

The Merivale group strolled out of the restaurant. Nick and Lori watched them go, then Nick turned to her with a worried expression.

"I never thought I'd agree with Gina Nichols about anything, but what she said is true, Lori. Tomorrow you do have to choose."

"I guess so," Lori agreed quietly. She couldn't even look up at him. "It's a hard choice, Nick," she said finally.

"It doesn't have to be, not if you follow your heart." He took her hand in his, willing her to look back up at him. Lori could see that there was so much he wanted to say. But he just couldn't find the right words.

"Hey, Hobart," one of his friends called out. "You coming with us, or what?"

Most of the Cougars were already gone, and Lori could see that Nick didn't want to be left behind.

"I'll catch up with you in a minute," Nick called back. Then he turned toward Lori again. "Think about what I said, Lori."

Lori just nodded as Nick bent to kiss her. He

walked away quickly, hurrying to catch up with his friends.

Nick and Gina are right. I thought I could just declare myself "neutral." But tomorrow I will have to choose a side.

CHAPTER NINE

Earlier on that Friday the excitement at both schools had built to fever-pitch. In Danielle's psychology class Mrs. Ellis had fought a losing battle, trying to hold her students' attention.

Danielle didn't like Mrs. Ellis very much, but she had to admire her teacher's persistence. After only one week of working at the day-care center, Danielle knew how it felt to be in Mrs. Ellis's position. During the past few days the student body at Atwood had been acting much like the preschoolers at the day-care center, Danielle thought.

Finally the bell rang, and there was a stampede to the door. Danielle was caught in the crush of bodies, but managed to step aside when she heard Mrs. Ellis call her name.

As Danielle worked back against the flow of traffic, she wondered what Mrs. Ellis had to say to her. Had Betsy Harper given her a poor report after all? If her grade hadn't been raised after all the time she had spent at the center, Danielle thought she'd scream.

"You wanted to speak to me?" Danielle asked, standing beside the teacher's desk.

Mrs. Ellis smiled and pushed her tortoise-shell glasses up on her head. "Your work at the day-care center is almost over, Danielle. How did you like it?"

"At first, I wasn't really wild about it," Danielle said honestly. "I guess Betsy Harper told you that."

"Yes, Betsy did say you seemed a bit out of your element the first day," Mrs. Ellis replied in an understanding tone.

"Well, I've never been around young children much, so it was hard. I didn't know how to talk to them or play with them," Danielle explained. "But after a while, it got easier. I kind of like hanging out with them now," Danielle admitted, surprising both herself and Mrs. Ellis.

"Betsy feels that you've been a great help to her with the children."

Danielle beamed. "Did she really say that?"

Mrs. Ellis nodded. "She told me that she's had a lot of high school volunteers, but you are by far the most—resourceful. Did you really bring your dog over there?"

Danielle grinned. "Garbo was a big hit. The kids really spoiled her with all their attention."

Danielle told Mrs. Ellis about a couple of the dog's antics. Her back was turned to the doorway, and she had no idea that Heather and Teresa were waiting for her. Waiting and, naturally, listening in on every word of Danielle and Mrs. Ellis's conversation.

"It sounds like you both had a vital learning experience," Mrs. Ellis said finally. "I just wanted you to know that I'm very pleased with the way you've handled this special assignment, Danielle. I'm going to give you an A on your work and average it in with your other test score."

Danielle breathed a heartfelt sigh of relief. "You mean I can raise my F?"

The teacher nodded.

"Wow, thanks, Mrs. Ellis." Danielle was smiling brightly. "You've really made my day. I have to run. I'll be late for history," she added as she headed for the door.

"Hurry then. Don't be late. See you at the game," the teacher replied. Danielle turned and stared at her.

"Like everyone else around here, I plan on watching the Cougars *trounce* Merivale tomorrow," Mrs. Ellis said, peering at Danielle with an uncharacteristic spark of mischief in her gaze.

"Way to go, Mrs. Ellis!" Danielle replied approvingly. "See you at the game!"

Danielle was still in a great mood later that day after history. She breezed down the corridor and spotted Teresa and Heather waiting at her locker. She guessed that they wanted to talk about the game—and of course, find out what she was going to wear.

Danielle couldn't help but notice that her friends were really treating her differently. They kept talking about how unselfish she was to work at the day-care center. The way they put her on a pedestal made Danielle feel a little uneasy. After all, she knew that she wasn't working at the center for totally *unselfish* reasons.

But Teresa and Heather didn't have to know that, she told herself. Danielle didn't even want to imagine what her friends would do and say. Teresa and Heather absolutely *despised* being tricked. Especially being tricked by Danielle.

"Hi, guys. I thought you two were going over to the mall to buy new outfits for the game tomorrow." Danielle put some books in her locker. Then she took out her leather jacket and a bag of candy she had bought for the kids. "I wish I could go shopping with you too. But duty calls—"

"Poor Danielle. What a saint," Teresa said snidely.

"She's so noble and unselfish," Heather said in the same sarcastic tone.

Danielle felt a shiver of apprehension race up her spine. But she willed herself to remain cool. Something was definitely up with Heather and Teresa.

"Okay—knock it off, you guys. It's just volunteer work. I've never claimed to be Florence Nightingale."

"Yeah—volunteer work that's going to get you a better grade in your psych class."

Danielle felt her face go white. How in the world had they found out? "What are you talking about?" she asked Teresa in an innocent tone.

"Don't play dumb with us, Danielle. We were standing outside of Mrs. Ellis's room before last period, and we heard *everything*."

"It took us a while, but we finally got to the bottom of your little act, Danielle. You thought you were making fools out of us for the past two weeks," Heather snarled. "But we knew something was going on."

"Wait a second," Danielle pleaded with them. "I know it looks like I was just trying to trick you, but I really do like working with those kids. I'd probably do it anyway—even if I wasn't trying to improve my grade—"

"Hah! That's a laugh," Heather cut in. "You would have never started working there if Mrs. Ellis hadn't forced you to, Danielle. And you know it. Why, you're the most *unlikely* candidate for volunteer work I know."

"Hey, wait a minute. That's not true—" Danielle argued back.

"Save your breath, Danielle. You had some nerve calling Heather and me shallow and selfish the other day. You beat us by a mile! If you think we're going to help you out with those kids at the mall, you're *crazy*. We never intended to go, did we, Heather?"

"No way! That was just a little trick we thought up," Heather added. "What a jerk you are to believe we'd actually do it!"

Danielle tossed back her head, sending a ripple of waves through her gorgeous red hair. "It doesn't matter to me one tiny bit if you come along or not. Betsy will go."

"*Sure*, Danielle." Teresa smirked. "This was *your* little field trip. Are you going to ask for help now? What will happen to your grade? It's not final yet, you know."

"Just wait until you're all alone with them at the mall. They'll go wild. You're going to run yourself ragged trying to keep up with them." Heather snickered.

Danielle knew that every word Heather and Teresa said was absolutely true. But she certainly wouldn't give them the satisfaction of agreeing with them.

"Listen, I'm going to the mall with those kids and we're going to have a great time. Now, if you'll get out of my way, I have to get to the center—"

"Oh, we wouldn't dream of standing in the *noble* volunteer's way! Would we, Heather?" Teresa said. They stepped aside so Danielle could pass.

Danielle could hear them laughing as she hurried down the crowded hall. She ran out to her car, climbed in, and gunned the engine, leaving a strip of rubber on the pavement.

Danielle fumed all the way over to the daycare center. She knew she shouldn't have lied to Teresa and Heather. But those two really asked for it sometimes. It was totally rotten of them to back out on the field trip. She couldn't call it off and disappoint the kids. But it was unlikely that she could find anyone to help her out now.

Asking Betsy was out of the question. And it was probably against the law to take ten kids on a field trip alone! She had to have another person with her, at least. Or take less kids.

Danielle was so distracted, she nearly forgot that she had to bring cookies and ice cream to the center. The mall was just up ahead, and she followed the steady stream of cars turning into the parking lot.

At Cookie Connection Danielle impatiently drummed her fingernails on the countertop as she waited for her turn. She recognized her cousin's tacky friend, Patsy Donovan, behind the counter, but she knew there was no way Patsy would ever give her special service.

Lori's friends positively hated her, and Danielle knew it. She, Teresa, and Heather had played quite a few mean tricks on Lori's group. Lori always forgave them, but not her friends. She and Lori certainly weren't close anymore, but Danielle knew that in a pinch, she could always turn to her cousin. Good old Lori would never let her down.

That's it! I'll ask Lori to help me with the kids. If I beg her, she'll probably say yes.

It was Danielle's turn next, and she ordered three dozen chocolate-chip cookies and a few half gallons of ice cream. Patsy handed the goods across the counter. "Don't get a bellyache now, Danielle," she said with forced sweetness.

Danielle smiled with saccharin sweetness and gave Patsy's considerable girth a telling glance. "Luckily, I don't have much of a belly to ache. Not like some people . . ."

Feeling satisfied at having had the last word, Danielle strolled out of the shop and headed down two doors to Tio's. Lori was sitting on a bench, just outside the restaurant. She was sipping a soda and staring vacantly in front of her. Danielle noticed that her cousin didn't look as if she was her usual cheerful self.

"Hi, Lori." Danielle sat down next to her on the bench. "What's new?"

Lori gave a listless shrug. "Not much. How about you?"

"I'm almost done with that day-care job I told you about. It looks like I'll do okay in the course after all."

"Well, that's great news. Congratulations. See, you were worried over nothing after all."

"Well, it's not over yet. I have to bring the kids to the mall on Monday for a field trip. But my two helpers just backed out on me. I can't handle them all by myself," Danielle said confidentially. "In fact, I'm not really allowed to."

Lori looked sympathetic, but Danielle could tell she wasn't about to volunteer her help. "Gee, that's too bad, Dani, but maybe you can find someone else to help you."

"Actually, Lori, I was wondering if you'd do it. As a *super* favor. I know how great you are with little kids, and it really wouldn't take up much time. And I'd be grateful to you forever," Danielle pleaded.

"I'd like to help you, Dani. Honest. But I have to work. Ernie agreed to give me Saturday off. I can't ask for any more time. Sorry."

"Oh, please," Danielle begged. "If this field trip goes badly, I might not get a good grade after all—"

Lori felt sorry for her cousin, even though she knew Danielle only acted nice to her when she wanted something. She would have helped her out if she was free. But she really needed her job and the money.

"How about Teresa or Heather? Wouldn't they help you out in an emergency?"

"Oh, forget them!" Danielle said vehemently. "Those two are so self-centered it's positively disgusting." Danielle sighed. Gathering up her packages she stood up again. "Well, I'd better get going before this ice cream melts. See you at the game tomorrow."

"Right," Lori said, forcing a smile. She was trying her best to sound upbeat. But she was so worried about the next day that she could hardly think straight.

Danielle tossed the ice cream and cookies in the back seat of her car and then headed for the day-care center. She was devastated. Lori had been her last hope!

CHAPTER TEN

Saturday morning, bright sunlight streamed through the pink curtains in Lori's bedroom. Without even lifting her head from the pillow, she could see that the sky was a brilliant, cloudless blue. It was the kind of autumn day that inspired songs and poetry—and naturally, football games.

Just thinking of the game, Lori groaned. The night before she had prayed for rain, a hailstorm, even a tornado. But no such luck. There was no chance of the Atwood-Merivale showdown being called on account of weather.

Lori flopped over onto her back and stared at the ceiling. She felt terrible. Her stomach hurt and she had a pounding headache. Would anyone possibly believe that she would miss the game with a case of the flu? *A convenient case of the flu. Suspiciously convenient*, she mumbled to herself.

If only I had thought ahead and broken my leg or something yesterday. There was just no way out of it. She had to go to the stadium and make her choice for the entire world to see.

Lori dragged herself out of bed and went into the bathroom. She brushed her teeth and washed her face. She looked at her reflection in the mirror, trying to force a smile. Big blue eyes stared back, her lips just barely curving upward in a courageous grin.

"By the time today is over, Randall," she told herself, "you might be a complete social outcast, or you might not have a boyfriend. But you'll always know that you *didn't* take the coward's way out—"

Suddenly there was a sharp knock on the bathroom door. "Lori?" her mother called. "Breakfast is almost ready. Are you coming down?"

"In a minute," Lori called back. She wondered if her mother had listened to her little pregame pep talk.

"It's french toast—your favorite," Mrs. Randall said.

Lori poked her head out the bathroom door and saw her pretty blond mother. "Gee, I didn't really feel hungry this morning, but I can't pass up french toast."

"I know you can't. I wanted to make sure you had a good breakfast this morning because you have a big day ahead of you." Her mother gave her a knowing smile. And Lori had an uncanny feeling that her mother knew more about what was happening than she let on.

"Oh, you mean with the game and all—"

"Mostly the 'and all' part." Lori's mother reached out and gently brushed a piece of hair from Lori's cheek. Then she turned and walked toward the stairs. "Hurry down, before your brothers get started. There won't be a crumb left."

Lori knew from experience her mother's words weren't just an idle threat. At ages eleven and eight, her two brothers were getting to the stage where they consumed everything in sight. She brushed out her hair and went down to the breakfast table in her bathrobe.

The french toast looked and smelled delicious, but every bite stuck in Lori's throat. Teddy, Mark, and her father, an elementary school principal, were talking about the game and trying to decide which side would win.

"Atwood's going to win," eight-year-old Mark said, his baseball cap pulled firmly down on his head. "They can't lose with Nick on their side." Mark simply idolized Nick. When Nick came to visit, Lori could hardly get her little brother to leave them alone for five minutes.

"Well, I worked out the statistics on my computer," Teddy announced, nodding his blond head. "Considering the win-loss records of both teams, and working in the temperature, wind speed, and humidity—it looks to me like Merivale has a winning edge."

"That sounds very scientific, Ted," Lori's father said, taking a sip of his coffee. "What about you, Lori? What's your guess?"

Lori glanced down at her plate, choosing her words carefully. "I don't know. I mean, the teams are so evenly matched."

Her father looked surprised at her response. "That's true. It would be impossible to say for sure. I was just wondering who you're going to cheer for. It's a tough one."

Tougher than you can imagine, Dad, Lori wanted to answer. Just then the phone rang and Lori's mother answered it. It was for Lori. She gratefully took the receiver, relieved at having an excuse to leave the breakfast table.

It was Ann, calling to say Ron had finished his paper and would be taking her to the game.

"We'll pick up Patsy too," Ann added. Lori didn't like the idea of going to the game without the moral support of her friends. But since the two girls lived close to each other, it made sense for Ann and Ron to pick up Patsy.

"If you get there first, try to save us seats, Lori. That is—if you're going to sit in the Merivale bleachers."

"I'll see you guys at the game then," Lori replied, not committing herself one way or the other. "Look for me."

After saying good-bye, Lori hung up the phone

and went up to her room. She slowly showered and did her hair and makeup. Then she dressed for the game in navy blue cords and an over-sized red- and blue-striped rugby shirt. She tied a big white pullover around her shoulders.

Later as Lori drove to the stadium, she felt as if a flock of butterflies had gone crazy in her stomach. If only Patsy and Ann had driven with her, she thought. Then she chided herself for being so babyish. The decision was hers, and nobody could really help her now.

The truth was Lori had already decided which side to sit on. Merivale High deserved her support. She adored Nick, but she felt a duty to her school. Even though she'd be cheering for Nick in her heart, Lori felt honor bound to take a seat in the Merivale bleachers.

As her red Spitfire slipped into a space in the Merivale Stadium parking lot, Lori's thoughts were centered on Nick. He'd feel hurt when he saw where she'd sat. *Will he even try to understand?* she wondered. *Why does love have to be so hard?*

Lori passed through the stadium gates and glanced around. The bleachers on either side of the field were filled, and music from both the Merivale and Atwood school bands competed for the spectators' attention.

As Lori entered, she felt people watching her, waiting to see which side she would choose. At first, she thought it was only her imagination.

Then she overheard two Atwood cheerleaders whispering about her.

"There's Lori Randall," the first one said. "I wonder if she's going to sit on our side."

"I hope she sits with Merivale, where she belongs," the other cheerleader said back. "Nick Hobart's sure to break up with her then. I'd go after that hunk *any day*."

The other girl laughed. "Get in line."

Lori's steps slowed as she thought. The girls' whispers stung. *They're right*, Lori thought. *Nick just might break up with me if I sit on the Merivale side*. "Let your heart decide," he had told her.

There are so many girls eager to go out with him if they had a chance. What am I doing walking to the Merivale bleachers? she wondered. *Am I crazy or what?*

She glanced up at the Atwood bleachers. There was her cousin Danielle. But the rest of the crowd looked awfully unfriendly. She just didn't feel she belonged with them.

Then she glanced over at the Merivale bleachers, filled with the familiar faces of her friends, classmates, and teachers.

That's where I really belong, Lori thought. *I just can't sit on the Atwood side. It wouldn't be right*. She walked to the opposite side of the field.

As Lori climbed the stairs into the Merivale bleachers, kids began talking to one another about her arrival. "All right, Randall!" one boy boldly called out. Other kids immediately joined in, cheering Lori on. On the other side of the field, the Atwood fans had noticed Lori cross to the other bleachers. They began to boo just as loudly as Merivale cheered.

Her face flame red, Lori soon located Patsy, Ron, and Ann. She wriggled through the crowded row and squeezed in beside them.

"Thanks for saving me a spot," she said.

"We saw you come in way over there," Ann said. "But for a second we thought you were going to sit on the Atwood side—"

"Well, here I am." Lori shrugged and gave her friends a wistful smile. "Win or lose—"

After the team introductions, the gun sounded and the Merivale Vikings kicked off. The entire stadium came to their feet in one huge roar. Lori didn't have another second to wonder if she was doing the right thing. The game had begun and she had made her choice.

During the first quarter, the Cougars moved over the Vikings like a steamroller. They couldn't do anything wrong, and every fumble seemed to roll their way. Nick was in full control as he called the plays and tossed one breathtaking pass after another. The score was soon Atwood, fourteen—Merivale, *nothing*!

The Merivale fans were furious. Every time the officials gave another call in Atwood's favor, they went absolutely crazy.

Then all of a sudden the Vikings came to life! They intercepted the ball at the start of the second quarter and ran it all the way down the field for a touchdown. The Merivale fans jumped up and down, roaring with new-found hope. Lori could feel the stands sway, as if the flimsy wood and metal structure couldn't hold up under the tremendous excitement.

The Cougars met the challenge boldly and got three more points. But, battling back just as hard, the Vikings managed to score another touchdown and the score was 17–14—Cougars.

From then on the teams fought neck and neck, battling with gritty intensity for every yard. By the middle of the second half the players looked exhausted. Lori's heart went out to them—*especially* to Nick, who looked as if he were ready to drop.

Lori wondered if Nick had noticed her. She couldn't tell for sure. She kept trying to catch his eye, to telegraph her support and encouragement. But he seemed to be concentrating totally on the game and didn't even glance her way.

Toward the end of the final quarter, Jack Baxter called a perfect "sneak play"—faking a pass and then running down field with the ball himself. The Vikings were within scoring distance to the end field and a three-point kick finally tied the score.

With only three minutes left to play, the embattled Cougars called a time out. Lori saw Nick run over to the sidelines for an emergency chat with his coach. Her heart ached for him. All the Atwood fans were counting on Nick now to push the Cougars over the top, just as he had done so many times before. They stomped their feet and chanted, "Hobart! Hobart! Hobart! Do it! Do it! Do it!"

Nick came back out on the field, and they roared. He pulled his helmet off and looked up at the stands. He wasn't just acknowledging the crowd's support, Lori realized, but searching the stands for one familiar face. He didn't seem to care that all the other players were waiting for him to finish the game.

"Oh, my gosh! I think Nick is looking for you, Lori!" Patsy whispered frantically.

Lori just didn't know what to do. She wanted to run out on the field and throw her arms around him, to tell him that he could win. She *knew* he could do it. But instead, she sat frozen in her seat as Nick's gaze slowly swung around to the Merivale stands.

Their eyes locked. Lori waved, but Nick didn't smile back. His expression became hard and stern. He yanked his helmet back on and slowly jogged out onto the field. She watched him huddle, then take his position in the formation.

Everything happened in a flash after that. Nick was going back with the ball, searching for someone to pass to. The Merivale stands shouted, "Sack! Sack! Sack the quarterback!"

One of the Vikings nicknamed Meat Locker

broke through the defensive line and hit Nick—hard. Gallantly Nick tried to pass the ball before he hit the ground. But the ball only spiraled straight into the air and never met its intended receiver. A Viking made an incredible leap, intercepted the pass, and ran madly down field. The Cougars followed in hot pursuit and bodies were hurled in all directions. Although the jersey was actually torn off his back, the Merivale player made it to the end zone and scored the winning touchdown just as the final gun sounded.

The Merivale fans roared and the Atwood fans let out a massive groan. Lori was stunned. For the first time in twenty years, Merivale had beaten Atwood! All around her, people went wild.

But all Lori could think about was Nick. While everyone else had been watching the final run, she had been watching Nick slowly pull himself up off the ground. She couldn't see the expression on his face, but his hanging head and drooping shoulders told the entire story.

The fans ran onto the field to congratulate their team. It was mayhem around the Vikings' bench. Gina Nichols was at the center of it all. She was simultaneously hugging Jack Baxter, waving a pom-pom, and letting out victory cheers.

"I want to congratulate some of the players—if I can fight my way through this crowd," Ann said. Ron stood up to join her.

"Yeah, they deserve a ticker-tape parade after that battle," Patsy added. "Are you coming, Lori?"

"You guys go ahead—I think I'll wait until the crowd thins out."

While the Vikings received the applause of their fans, the Atwood crowd filed out of the stadium, as solemn as people in a funeral procession. Lori ran across the field and searched for Nick. He was sitting alone on a bench with his head in his hands. He looked utterly dejected, his uniform ripped and mud stained. Lori ran to him. She tentatively reached out and touched his shoulder. *I'd do anything right now to make Nick feel better. Anything.*

"Nick," Lori whispered. "Please, don't feel so bad. It was just a game. Not the end of the world—"

But Nick barely lifted his head to glance at her. He shrugged off her hand as if he couldn't bear her touch.

"Go away," he replied in a gruff, strained voice. "You didn't want to help me when I needed you—and I don't need your pity now, Lori."

Nick's words stung Lori. "I'm sorry, Nick. I only did what *I* thought was right."

He lifted his head and glared at her. "But you weren't for *me*. That's all I know. When I looked for you, you weren't there. I kind of lost my head when I saw you sitting on the Merivale side. I couldn't concentrate anymore. If only you'd been here, I wouldn't have fumbled the ball like that—"

What was he saying? Was he really blaming *her* because Atwood lost the game?

"Nick, please, you can't blame me for what happened—" Lori pleaded. "It was just an unlucky break. It certainly isn't my fault Atwood lost—"

"Don't you see, Lori? You betrayed me. To me, it was as if you ran out on the field and knocked that ball out of my hand yourself."

His beautiful aquamarine eyes were red rimmed, filled with tears. Lori felt her heart being torn in two.

"Nick, I *never* betrayed you. I wanted you to play your best—and win—with all my heart. You've got to believe me," Lori implored him.

Nick came to his feet with a sad, harsh laugh. "It's fine to say that now, Lori. You can say *anything* now. But actions speak louder than words. If you really loved me, you'd have gone the limit for me. You'd have sat with Atwood." Nick tucked his helmet under his arm. "You don't care about me. That's the bottom line."

"You can't believe that, Nick!" Lori felt tears well up in her eyes. She felt her whole world crumbling around her. And there was nothing she could do to stop it. "Of course I care about you. I'd do anything for you. Anything at all."

Lori stared into Nick's eyes, wishing she could

reach out and take his hand. But she didn't dare move even a step closer to him.

For one brief moment she thought there was a flicker of sympathy in his gaze. She held her breath, silently praying he would listen to her.

Then his expression hardened again. "There's nothing you can do for me *now*, Lori. I lost a lot more out there today than a football game." Nick gazed out at the empty field. "Face it, you don't care about our relationship. I think it's time we broke up."

Lori was crushed. She felt as if she'd just had the wind knocked out of her. "You really want to break up?" she asked quietly.

Nick stared down at the ground. Finally he just nodded. Lori could see that nothing she might say or do would make a difference then.

"Okay, then, if that's what you want," Lori managed to say. "Good-bye, Nick—"

She turned away and began to walk across the field. She hoped Nick would change his mind and run after her. But he didn't. Her vision blurred with tears. Lori turned around once to look at him. He was shuffling slowly in the opposite direction.

CHAPTER ELEVEN

"I want popcorn!"

"I want licorice!"

"I don't want to sit next to Jeremy. He smells funny—"

"Okay, you'll all have popcorn once we get inside. Now hold hands and stay together," Danielle said. She and the six older preschoolers, who Betsy said she could take on her own, had just entered the mall and were on their way to the six-plex to see a Disney movie. Literally swept along on the tide of eager children, Danielle was not at all sure she was going to survive the afternoon.

In front of the theater Danielle did her eighth quick head count since driving into the mall. The kids were in constant motion, so Danielle had assigned each of them a "buddy" and warned them all not to lose sight of each other.

During the week Danielle had stopped by a

police-awareness booth in the mall to read some pamphlets about safeguarding children against strangers and kidnappers. Danielle found them interesting at the time. But now that she was in charge of six kids on her own, she suddenly realized what an awesome responsibility she had taken on.

Good thing we're going to the movies. At least they'll all be sitting in one place at one time. And I can keep my eye on them.

Danielle happily paid for the movie tickets and supervised the short parade of children as they filed through the turnstile.

In the theater's huge lobby, two kids ran off. The others stood quietly holding hands as they waited for popcorn and candy.

Danielle yelled at the four kids not to move, and then ran after the other two. One was at the water fountain, the other in a line for a detective film. As she yanked him away, she heard a familiar laugh.

"Well, if it isn't Merivale's answer to Mr. Rogers! What a surprise!" Teresa simpered.

"How's life in 'Romper Room' today, Danielle?" Heather chimed in.

"I'm having a *lot* of fun," Danielle answered coolly. She was holding a squirming little boy in each hand. "It certainly beats doing the same old boring things with the same old *boring* people," she replied.

Teresa and Heather laughed snidely. "Well,

enjoy the movie. We're going up to Facades afterward," said Heather.

"They're having a *private* sale for select customers," Teresa said in a tantalizing tone. "Too bad you can't join us, Danielle."

A private sale at Facades! How could she miss it? Danielle was consumed with envy inside. But she certainly wouldn't let Teresa and Heather know. She shrugged indifferently.

"Who wants last season's leftovers? I'm going to New York next weekend—to shop at some *real* stores," Danielle replied. "See you later, girls."

Her mother actually had no plans to take Danielle shopping in New York, but Danielle didn't give that small detail a thought. Pleased at having gotten the last word with Teresa and Heather, she took off after the other children and bought them all popcorn.

Danielle herded the kids into the theater and found seven empty seats in a row. She sighed when they were finally all seated. *Thank goodness I can sit back and relax,* she thought.

But even before the Coming Attractions were over, the children began to get rambunctious again. They were crawling on the floor, throwing popcorn at one another, and bouncing on the seats as if they were trampolines. The darkness made it very difficult for Danielle to control them.

Some other people in the theater soon began

complaining. Danielle cringed with embarrassment as people spoke to her.

"Excuse me, miss," one older woman whispered, "but I paid good money to bring my grandchildren here, and those little rowdies are spoiling everything!"

"I'm really sorry," Danielle whispered back. "They're just a little excited right now. They'll calm down in a minute," she promised.

They'd better calm down—and fast. She didn't want the usher to throw them all out. Then what would she do with them?

Danielle spent the next hour apologizing with one breath and reprimanding the children in a hoarse whisper with the next. The only way she had of controlling them was to withhold popcorn and candy from those who misbehaved. They were still pretty rowdy for the rest of the movie—but not *completely* outrageous.

When the movie was over, Danielle herded them out to the lobby. After sitting through an entire movie, the kids were bursting with pent-up energy. Danielle, however, felt completely drained. But she still had another hour left to entertain them! Why were Disney movies so short?

This has to be the longest day of my life. Why did I ever leave school early to do this? I must be crazy, Danielle said to herself.

"What are we going to do now?" one little girl asked, tugging on Danielle's pants. "I'm bored!"

"I'm hungry," a little boy named Billy said as he tugged on Danielle's other leg.

"I'm thirsty," an adorable five-year-old named Kristi Ingram said.

Danielle put her hands on her head and nearly screamed out loud with frustration. "All right, you guys, listen up!" she yelled out like a drill sergeant. "I want everyone to find their buddy and hold hands." She waited while the six kids paired off. Finally, they were in a sort of two-by-two line. "Okay, we're going to take a nice walk around the mall now."

"Where are we going?" one boy asked.

"Uh—that's a surprise. You'll just have to follow me and find out," Danielle said in a tantalizing voice. "And you better behave. Or no surprise."

She really had no idea where they would end up or what the surprise was going to be. But the kids didn't have to know that, she reminded herself. With the promised "surprise" dangling before them like a carrot on a stick, they were already acting more orderly.

Danielle led the group around the first level and stopped beside a man selling silver helium balloons in front of the fountain. She bought one for each child. As they paraded around, Danielle realized that the six silver balloons made her group look even *more* conspicuous.

I'm never going to hear the end of this at school, she realized with a sudden shudder.

After the balloons, Danielle bought them all chocolate-chip cookies at Cookie Connection. She didn't have the vaguest notion of what to do with them next. She was at her wit's end and almost out of money, and the kids were getting wild again. Forty-five minutes to fill!

"Give Nick some time, Lor. I'm sure he didn't really mean he wanted to break up," Ann said, trying to comfort her friend.

"He was just angry and feeling lousy about losing the game," Patsy added. "He needs time to think things over."

Lori was due at work in a few minutes, but Patsy and Ann had persuaded her to browse through some clothes stores first, hoping it would lift her spirits. They had whisked through the racks at Snazzz! and were now trying to find an empty dressing room at Mon Cheré. Ann had persuaded Lori to try on a red suede mini dress and when they finally found an empty room and Lori put it on, her friends were awed.

"Gosh, Lori, that dress was made for you. You look fabulous!" Patsy said.

"Red is definitely your color," Ann agreed.

Lori shook her head. "I think I'll pass," she said, pulling down the zipper.

Lori really appreciated her friends' efforts to cheer her up. But she still didn't feel the slightest bit better. After the game on Saturday and all day Sunday she had cried. Lori knew she looked simply dreadful and had almost called in sick to school and work. But she just couldn't.

"I don't think Nick is going to change his mind," Lori said with a wistful sigh as they walked out of Mon Cheré. "I called him last night. I was afraid to, but I thought maybe he wasn't angry anymore."

"What happened?" Ann asked excitedly.

Lori shook her head. "He wouldn't even speak to me. . . ." Lori's throat felt tight and tears suddenly filled her huge blue eyes. "He just hates me now." She sniffed.

"Of course he didn't talk to you—yet. But that doesn't mean he hates you. Nick just needs time to cool off," Ann said as they got on the down escalator.

"Oh, my gosh! I must be hallucinating! Look at that!" Patsy said, pointing down to the first level. Lori and Ann turned to look. "Over there—I think your cousin Danielle has been taken hostage by a half-dozen preschoolers!"

Ann started laughing and covered her mouth with her hand. "I can't believe it. Danielle and all those little kids! They look pretty wild. Maybe Patsy is right. Maybe they are holding Danielle for ransom."

The sight of her cousin trying to lead the group of children through the mall made even Lori smile. *Poor Danielle.* She really did need help, Lori thought. But obviously, she hadn't been able to enlist anyone to come to her rescue. "She's been working at a day-care center as a volunteer," Lori explained to her friends.

"Danielle? *Volunteering?*" Ann echoed in utter disbelief. "I know she's your cousin, Lori, but I've never heard of Danielle voluntarily helping anyone out."

It was too bad Danielle gave people such a rotten impression, Lori thought. There really was a side to her cousin that was brave and caring. But most people only saw Danielle as gorgeous, self-centered, and very willful. It was impossible for Lori to even try to defend her cousin.

"The volunteer work is a project for her psychology class," Lori explained as they stepped off the escalator. "But Danielle really likes it."

"I'll bet," Ann scoffed. "Just look at her. She looks like she's ready to tear her hair out."

Danielle certainly did look frazzled. Lori had to agree.

"Hey, this is the best joke I've heard all week. Danielle Sharp, baby-sitting for a pack of whiny little kids."

"I'm going over to say hello," Lori said. "Be back in a second." Even though Lori wasn't in the mood for Danielle's usual barbs, she couldn't let her cousin pass by without giving her a few words of encouragement.

"Hey, Danielle! How's it going?" Lori called out as she ran up to the group.

"Bobby, get down from there! You're going

to fall into the fountain!" Danielle nabbed one little boy by the collar and gently helped him off the ledge that rimmed the bubbling fountain. Another little girl with blond curls and a face smeared with ice cream was crying and pulling on Danielle's sweater. "Oh, Lori! Hi! What's the matter now, Charlotte?" Danielle asked the little girl in the same breath.

"You look like you have your hands full. I just wanted to say hello."

"Don't go, Lori," Danielle pleaded. "I haven't spoken to anyone over the age of five for hours. I *never* in a million years thought it would be this awful," Danielle moaned. "I should have my head examined for volunteering to do this dumb trip! I don't know what else to do with them. I have them until six o'clock. I'll never make it!"

"You're not doing so badly," Lori told her. "Why don't you take them over to Video Arcade? That should distract them for a while."

"Of course! Why didn't I think of that before— Hey, who wants to play some video games?" she shouted over the din of voices.

"Me! Me first!" The kids jumped up and down with excitement.

"Okay, let's go! Don't worry, you'll all get to play," she promised them.

They all charged off in the direction of the arcade as Danielle managed to do a quick head count. *They were all still there, thank goodness. Only one half hour left to go. . . .*

When they got inside the arcade, Danielle

bought tokens for all and pressed them into the children's hot, eager little hands. Finally, she reached the last little girl in line, Kristi Ingram. "Remember, stay with your buddy," she reminded her.

The arcade was packed and unbelievably noisy. The children took their game tokens and lined up at the two nearest machines. Danielle told them not to move from those games until they all went as a group.

The arcade echoed with the wild sounds of ringing, buzzing, and shouting. It was hardly an ideal place to relax and clear your mind. Danielle would have liked to step outside and check out some boutique windows. But she didn't dare leave the kids on their own for even a second.

She was called just then to help Kristi reach the controls on Hyper Space.

"Well, look who's here—I never knew you were into Hyper Space," a deep voice behind her said.

Danielle whirled around and was grateful for the dark so Don James couldn't see her blush. As usual, he was wearing his worn leather jacket, black T-shirt, and jeans. And as usual, he took her breath away. But that day she had no time to worry about how he affected her.

"Don! What a surprise." Danielle gave him a hundred-watt smile. She didn't even care if people saw them together. She needed to talk to a full-grown person before her brain turned to mush.

"Danielle, can I have more tokens?" Billy tugged on her sleeve. Danielle gave him a few more game tokens and the little boy skipped away.

"Uh-oh, looks like you're here with friends," Don said, teasing her.

"The kids from the day-care center. I was dumb enough to volunteer to take them out for the afternoon," Danielle explained.

"Looks like they're having a great time," Don said.

"Oh, *they* are," Danielle agreed. "I'm the one who's going crazy."

At that moment Kristi pulled her hand. "Danielle, will you help me play Hyper Space again? I can't reach the buttons. I'm too little."

Danielle sighed out loud. "I'm talking to my friend right now, Kristi. I'll be there in a minute."

"But I want to play *now*." Kristi pouted. "Please—pretty please."

Hearing Kristi whine, Danielle felt her frayed nerves snap. "I'm busy. Just play that game next to it. You can reach that one."

"Okay—" With her head bent down, Kristi dragged her feet and moved away.

Danielle quickly brushed the guilty feeling aside. She had been spoiling the kids for the past couple of hours. She had given them whatever they wanted. There was no reason for her to feel guilty about talking to Don for a minute.

Don bought Danielle a diet soda and they stood where they could still see the kids. After a couple of minutes she looked at her watch and sighed. It was almost six o'clock. She could round up the children. It was almost time for their parents to pick them up.

"I'd better start prying these kids away from the machines. Their parents are meeting us at six," Danielle told Don.

"Good luck," Don said. "They don't look too eager to leave, but then I wouldn't want to leave you either."

"Bye, Don," Danielle replied.

"See you around, Red." He looked down at her, his face only inches from hers.

"See you, Don," she said, held by his gaze. Finally she broke away to pick up her charges.

"Okay, kids. We're ready to leave now. Make sure you don't forget anything—sweaters, dolls, your balloons," she said, reminding them. The idea of running back and hunting around for a lost stuffed animal or jacket did not appeal to her.

When they got out into the mall, Danielle decided to do one last head count, just to be sure no one had been left behind. "Everybody hold your buddy's hand now," she told them as she casually looked over the group.

There had to be something wrong. She only counted five kids. Danielle counted again.

Only five! She had lost one of them! Kristi Ingram!

CHAPTER TWELVE

"Danielle?" Charlotte looked up at her. "I don't have a buddy anymore. Will you hold my hand?"

Danielle was frantic. She hardly heard what the little girl was saying.

"Charlotte," she said calmly, although her heart was pounding alarmingly fast. "Where's Kristi? It's very important that you remember."

"Um—I don't know." Charlotte shrugged. "She has my balloon."

Kristi had just been there. She couldn't have gotten far. But where could she be? Maybe she sneaked back inside the arcade. Danielle's pulse was racing. She squeezed her eyes closed. "Please let her be in there," she whispered under her breath.

When she opened her eyes, she saw Don standing beside her again. "You guys still hanging out here? I thought you'd be long gone by now," he said, greeting Danielle and the children in a friendly tone.

"Oh, Don! You've got to help me," Danielle pleaded. "Please stay with the kids a second while I run back inside."

"Sure. Forget something?"

"Yes!" Danielle wailed as she flew back toward the arcade. "Kristi Ingram is missing! I just hope she's still in there—"

She ran back into the dark, noisy arcade and searched up and down the aisles, mistaking every shadow for the missing Kristi. She asked everyone if they had seen a little blond-haired girl wandering by herself. But nobody had. They all just shrugged and went back to their video games. Danielle looked in the rest room and the snack bar, but Kristi was nowhere.

She pressed her hands to her flushed cheeks, feeling as though she were going to cry. It was all her fault. When Kristi came over and asked her for help, she should have gone. They were her responsibility, and she had goofed up.

What should I do? Where can I go for help? Danielle asked herself. Then she remembered the booth the police had set up for information about missing children. Maybe somebody there could help her.

Outside in the mall, she stopped again to talk to Don. "Kristi isn't in there," Danielle told him breathlessly. "Nobody even remembers seeing her. I'm going over to that police booth to ask for help—"

"Good idea," Don called after her. "Don't worry about the kids. I'll stay with them until their parents come. Where are they to be picked up?"

"Fountain," was all Danielle called back before she dashed off to the kidnapping-awareness booth. There was a friendly policewoman inside who tried to calm her down as she listened to her story.

"I'm going to call the security office," the policewoman told Danielle. "If someone found the little girl, she'd be brought there. If not, the security staff will help you look for her."

Danielle waited tensely for the brief phone call to be over. *If only I'd been more careful*, she kept scolding herself.

The policewoman hung up the phone and turned back to Danielle. "They're going to begin a search immediately. But this mall is huge. It might take some time before she's found."

Danielle was beside herself with panic. She couldn't bear to wait to find Kristi. What was she going to tell the little girl's parents when they came to collect her? Danielle quickly thanked the policewoman for her help, then rushed back out into the mall.

Danielle decided to check all the places that might appeal to a child. First, she went up to the third level to Puppy Paradise. All kids loved watching puppies frisking around in their cages. Maybe she'd come and gone inside, Danielle thought.

Danielle dashed into the pet store. It was crowded with shoppers. Dogs were barking and birds chattered in their cages overhead. Danielle ran up to a salesman and described Kristi. He looked sympathetic but rushed. "Sorry—I see so many kids all day in here, it's hard to say," he told Danielle. "Why don't you go to the manager's office and ask them to page her on the PA?"

"Great idea!" Danielle rushed into the office and explained her problem. The manager was very obliging and immediately made the announcement. But after a few minutes it was obvious that Kristi wasn't in the store. Danielle's rush of hope disappeared. Thanking the store manager, she ran back down to the first level.

She stopped and asked the man selling balloons if he had seen her. He was sympathetic, but didn't remember Kristi.

Cookie Connection and the movie theater were also dead ends for Danielle. She didn't even bother going inside the movie house. Kristi didn't have any money to buy a ticket.

Outside the movie theater, Danielle met with a group of security guards. But they didn't have any good news. "We're doing everything we can, miss," one of the guards assured her. "But we've got four levels to cover, and she could be anywhere."

Feeling worse than ever, Danielle continued hunting for Kristi. This time she stopped in every single shop between the movie theater and the arcade. Kristi just had to be there someplace, Danielle kept telling herself. She just *had* to be.

Finally Danielle was back at Video Arcade. Still no sign of the missing little girl. Don and the other children were gone too. At the fountain or on their way home with their parents.

Danielle dropped wearily onto a bench. She imagined poor little Kristi, wherever she was right then, scared and lost. *And it's all my fault,* Danielle scolded herself. Her mother will be here any second, and what'll I say?

Danielle hid her face in her hands and started to cry. She had never faced such a serious problem before. She knew she was sometimes self-centered and not as responsible as she could be. But right then Danielle promised herself that if she ever got out of this jam, she would do everything she could to change. If only Kristi weren't kidnapped! The very thought made Danielle start weeping again.

She didn't know how long she'd been sitting on the bench, when suddenly she felt a light tap on her knee.

"Why are you sad, Danielle?" a little girl asked her. "Don't cry. Do you want a balloon? I have two."

Danielle slowly lifted her head. At first, she thought she had to be dreaming. She blinked. It was true! It was really Kristi—safe and sound!

Danielle jumped off the bench and scooped her up. She had to make sure the little moppet was for real. "I can't believe it! You're really here! You're all right!"

Danielle was breathless with relief. For a second she thought she might even faint. She spun around and squeezed Kristi in her arms, afraid that the child might disappear into thin air again.

"I sure wish somebody would act that happy to see me," Don said, standing off to one side.

Danielle spun around. She realized that Don must have been watching her the entire time. Their eyes met, and Danielle felt the same exciting shiver race up her spine.

"Did *you* find her?" she asked him, continuing to clutch Kristi to her.

He nodded. "A friend of mine stayed with the other kids while I went to look."

"But I looked everywhere," Danielle said. "No one had seen her."

"Right—nobody saw her. She's so little she snuck under the turnstile at the six-plex and went back to the Disney movie."

"Was she crying? Was she afraid to be alone?" Danielle asked worriedly.

"Are you kidding?" Don laughed. "The only time she got upset was when I told her we had to leave. She never saw the ending the first time because all the other kids were so noisy." Don reached over and ruffled Kristi's hair. "Don't worry about this kid. She wasn't scared for a second. She didn't even know she was lost."

"Thank goodness you decided to check there," Danielle replied.

Don shook his head. "What a zoo! I was almost afraid to go inside—all those wild little kids jumping around."

"Don! You? A big tough guy? Don't tell me that's all just an act!" Danielle said, teasing him. "I'd be very disappointed—"

"I'd *never* disappoint you, Red," Don promised her with a wink.

Before Danielle could think of a snappy reply, Kristi squirmed in her arms. "Can I get down now? I think I see my mommy."

Smiling briefly, Mrs. Ingram walked up to them and gave Kristi a big kiss. "Hello, sweetheart. Did you have a nice day?"

Kristi nodded. "We played video games and had cookies. Look at my balloon—" She bubbled enthusiastically.

"How pretty," her mother said, admiring the heart-shaped silver balloon.

"And I went to the movies—twice," Kristi added.

Danielle held her breath and exchanged a worried glance with Don. Was Kristi going to tell her mother that she was lost? As Don said, the little girl never even realized that people were searching all over for her.

Danielle didn't know whether or not to tell Mrs. Ingram what had happened. She didn't know what purpose it would serve to worry

Kristi's mother now, especially since everything had turned out for the best. Finally it was Don who solved the problem for her.

"Kristi had some exciting day," he told Mrs. Ingram. "She gave us a scare there for a few minutes—"

"Gave you a scare?" Mrs. Ingram asked.

"Nothing serious. She just wandered back into the movies without telling anyone," Don explained calmly. "But she won't do that ever again, will you?" he asked, giving the little girl a stern look.

"Nope," Kristi said, shaking her head. "Did you see my balloon, Mommy?" she asked her mother again.

"Yes, dear. Very pretty." Mrs. Ingram took Kristi's little hand. "Well, good-bye now. And thank you again. I know you must have had your hands full, entertaining the children."

"Um—there were some hectic moments," Danielle admitted, avoiding Don's gaze.

After Kristi and her mother walked away, Danielle breathed an audible sigh of relief. She collapsed on the bench, and Don sat down next to her. Neither of them spoke for a long while.

"I don't know how to thank you, Don," Danielle said finally. "It seems like you're always bailing me out of trouble."

Don slipped his sunglasses on and pushed up the collar of his leather jacket. "By day, a mild-mannered but totally hip student and part-time auto mechanic," he crooned in deep voice. "But when trouble strikes in Merivale Mall—it's a bird, it's a plane—no, it's Super James." He whisked off his sunglasses and smiled a slow, infectious grin. "At your service, ma'am."

Danielle laughed. "How can I ever thank you for finding Kristi?"

Don raised his eyebrows. "Hmmm—you don't really want me to answer that question, Red." His dark eyes glittered dangerously.

Danielle just smiled, but inside, she felt that strange excitement that Don always inspired.

"Hmmm—maybe I don't," she replied coolly. "Then again, maybe you'd rather not hear what I'd have to say after your answer," Danielle added, taunting him.

CHAPTER THIRTEEN

"Hi, I'm home," Lori announced, swinging through the front door on Monday night. Nobody answered. She found a note from her mother on the kitchen table; it was propped up against the pepper mill. The note said her parents had taken her brothers to the movies, and there was barbecued chicken in the refrigerator for her if she was hungry.

Lori tossed the note on the counter and opened the refrigerator. She bypassed the chicken and poured herself a tall glass of cranberry-apple juice, which she sipped as she went upstairs to her room. After slipping on her long terry cloth bathrobe, Lori stretched out on the floor to look at a new French fashion magazine. One of her favorite albums was on the stereo.

Gee, it's great to have the house all to myself. It's so peaceful, she thought, leafing through the glossy pages. But a few moments later the quiet began to get on her nerves. The lack of distracting noise—like a TV blasting, or her brothers arguing with each other—gave Lori too much time to think. And her thoughts were only of Nick. The next song on her album was an even more sentimental reminder of him.

Her chin resting on her hand, Lori sighed, long and loud. She stared into space without turning a page of the magazine for a long time. When the song was over, the stereo shut itself off, and the quiet overwhelmed her.

Lori got up, but instead of turning the record over, as she had intended, she picked up the telephone and dialed Nick's number. *I'm thinking about him so much tonight, maybe he's thinking about me too*, she told herself. As she heard the phone ring on the other end of the line, she crossed her fingers.

Finally somebody at Nick's house picked up the phone. Lori immediately recognized his mother's voice. "Hi, Mrs. Hobart, this is Lori. Is Nick around?" she asked hopefully.

"Hi, Lori. Could you hold on just a moment, dear?" Mrs. Hobart said in her usual, friendly tone. Lori heard her cover the phone with her hand. A second later she came back on the line. "Lori, I'm sorry. Nick isn't home right now."

Lori felt her heart drop. "Oh, well, could you just tell him I called?"

"I'll make sure he gets the message, Lori. Good night."

"Good night," she said. As Lori hung up the phone, she realized that she was blinking back tears. *I'd better face it, he just doesn't want to have anything to do with me. And that's the absolute last time I'm going to call him,* she promised herself as she wiped her eyes.

Just then, Lori heard her parents and brothers come in. "Lori? Are you home?" her mother called from the bottom of the stairs.

"Up here," she called back.

"Come on down," her father said. "We brought back some of that homemade ice cream from Wessel's. You'd better hurry before your brothers inhale it—carton and all," he warned her.

"I'll be right there," Lori said. She splashed her face with cold water and combed out her hair. She knew that Nick wouldn't call her back when he got home. She even doubted that he was out of the house when she had called. *No, he won't call tonight,* she thought. *He'll probably never call me ever again.*

The next day, Tuesday, Atwood students had only half a day of school because of a teachers' conference. When the dismissal bell rang at noon, Danielle dumped her books in her locker and hopped into her car, heading straight to the mall. For more than a week she hadn't been able to hang out after school. No shopping or working out at the Body Shoppe. But that day she was back in action, and she couldn't wait.

How did I ever stand it? she wondered. *Not only was I away from the mall and all my friends, but I was stuck with those kids all afternoon.* It had been much worse than being grounded by her parents. No matter what her parents *said*, they always forgot she was being punished and, after a day or two, let her come and go as she pleased.

Oh, well. That's over now, thank goodness. I have a better grade in psych, and I don't have to worry about it anymore. As she drove toward the mall, Danielle couldn't decide where she'd go first. Up to Facades? Danielle thought she certainly deserved a new outfit after all she'd been through. Or perhaps to To the Manor Born, to have a manicure? Maybe Heather and Teresa would be there.

I need some new tapes too, Danielle remembered. *I can't forget to stop by Platterpuss Records. There's always somebody worthwhile hanging out there—*

Danielle screeched into a parking spot and quickly checked her reflection in the rearview mirror. She ran a comb through her luxurious hair and added some blush to her high cheekbones. She knew she looked great—but she wanted to look perfect for her first day back in circulation.

Danielle sailed gaily into the mall. She had hours to pamper herself and decided to start at the top and work her way down. As she rode the chrome and glass escalators all the way to the mall's fourth level, she glanced around for familiar faces. She made an appointment at To the Manor Born to have her nails done at four o'clock. Then she strolled through the gilded doors of Facades with regal flair. All the saleswomen greeted her warmly.

"Oh, Miss Sharp!" one of them said. "We missed you yesterday during our private sale."

"I wanted to stop in, but I was busy with something. A school assignment," Danielle said.

"Too bad," the saleswoman said sympathetically. "But I suppose there are more important things in life than shopping—"

"Really? For instance?" Danielle joked.

The saleswoman laughed. "When you're done looking at those dresses, see me," she added in a hushed tone. "I've tucked away something in suede that I think is just *perfect* for you."

Danielle tried on piles of clothes in styles that ranged from country-chic to haute couture. She was itching to buy herself something as a special treat. But as she gazed at her reflection dressed in one outfit after another, nothing seemed to strike her that day.

"What did you think of that purple leather Italian mini?" the saleswoman asked, poking her head into the dressing room. "I thought it would look just super on you."

Danielle shrugged. "It was all right, I guess," she said unenthusiastically as she checked out the back view in a black jumpsuit.

"You look divine in that." The saleswoman practically oozed. "Black has so much drama. It's the perfect backdrop for your stunning coloring, dear."

Danielle took another look at herself and frowned. Usually, she adored outfits like it. But that day, she thought she looked like a very stylish paratrooper.

"Hmmm—I don't think so," Danielle said, yanking open the snap-up front.

The saleswoman frowned. "Just call me if you need any help," she said. Like a turtle pulling its head into its shell, she disappeared and the dressing room door snapped closed.

Danielle reached for the next outfit in the pile, then decided instead to put her own clothes back on. She just wasn't in the mood to shop.

Out in the mall once more, she checked her watch. Already three o'clock? If she hurried, she could take the three-fifteen aerobics class at the Body Shoppe. Danielle dashed over to the posh fitness club and changed into a pink- and blue-striped leotard in record time.

Ann Larson was teaching the class and had begun with some gentle stretching exercises to warm up. Danielle took a place in the back and joined in. As she followed Ann's instructions, her thoughts wandered. She thought of what she would be doing right then at the day-care center. Maybe she'd be outside, leading a game of Bluebird, or reading the children a story.

They loved the way she read and used different voices and faces for each of the characters.

"Okay, ladies. Now we're going to do some work on those saddlebags," Ann said brightly. "Please roll on your side, with your head propped on your hand like this." Ann demonstrated the position. "Danielle? Is something the matter?" Ann asked, interrupting the class.

Danielle realized that she was still doing the last exercise while everyone had gone on to something else. "I'm fine," she said, quickly getting into the same position as the rest of the class.

Time to work on those minor imperfections, she reminded herself, concentrating totally on the exercise. *Priorities, Danielle! Working on your hips is definitely more important than worrying about those dumb little kids.*

When the class ended, Teresa and Heather walked over to Danielle. She hadn't even noticed they were there. "Well, look who's decided to grace us with her presence," Teresa said, simpering.

"Where are your little friends today, Dani?" Heather asked, glancing around. "Couldn't they come out and play?"

"Very funny," Danielle said. She patted her forehead with a fluffy white towel. She was torn between defending her attachment to the day-care children and trying to get back into her regular routine—which inevitably meant calling a truce with Teresa and Heather. "So, how was the private sale at Facades yesterday? Find anything good?" she asked finally.

Having just left the store herself, she didn't really feel like talking about shopping. But she knew the subject would get her friends talking to her in the usual way again. Teresa and Heather both started chattering at once about all the wonderful clothes they'd bought. Danielle sighed enviously whenever she thought it was necessary.

When it was time for her manicure, Danielle went back up to the beauty salon. She was ushered in immediately and sat facing her favorite manicurist across the small table.

"What have you been doing with these hands!" Lana, the manicurist, exclaimed. "Working on your car? Digging turnips?"

"Oh, come on, Lana. They're not that bad," Danielle said lightly. While playing with the children, Danielle had to put her perfect nails through all sorts of abuse. Her polish got chipped every day, and she'd broken almost every nail, but she hadn't really thought much about it. A little chipped polish seemed a small price to pay for all the fun she had had.

"Well, sit back and relax. It's going to take me a while to get these hands back in shape." Lana fussed as she applied an emery board to Danielle's pinky with an expert's touch. "I hope you're finished doing whatever you did to make them such a mess."

"Um—sure. It was just this dumb project for school. But I'm finished with it," Danielle replied. But instead of sounding happy and relieved about it, she heard her voice sounding almost sad.

A manicure usually lifted Danielle's spirits. But that day it seemed to have the opposite effect. She thanked Lana and gave her a generous tip for an excellent job.

As Danielle rode the escalator down to the first level, she was careful not to bump her newly painted nails. Since she hadn't worried about such a trivial matter for a while, it felt kind of strange.

Being honest with herself, Danielle had to admit that the entire afternoon had been less fun than she'd expected. For some reason, none of her usual pastimes were making her happy. She didn't understand why.

Junk food! That's what I need. My body is craving some totally non-nutritious Merivale Mall munchies. No wonder I don't feel right. I'm in a state of junk-food deprivation, Danielle diagnosed. She decided to stop at the first fast-food place she passed, which happened to be Tio's Tacos.

Danielle walked up to the counter, where her cousin Lori was busy at work. Why was Lori always so annoyingly productive and responsible? It was downright abnormal, Danielle thought crossly. Then she caught herself. Hadn't she looked pretty much the same way to Heather and Teresa when they'd seen her working at the day-care center?

The cousins greeted each other and Danielle ordered a taco and a diet soda.

"So how are you doing?" Lori asked while they were waiting for the food. "You must be happy that you don't have to work at the day-care center anymore."

"Yeah, what a drag. I couldn't wait for it to be over so I could hang out again," Danielle said. "Well, it wasn't really *that* bad," she added, thinking of the way the little kids had showered her with affection.

Lori looked at her curiously. "You almost sound as if you miss going there. Do you?"

Nestled in its cardboard box, the taco glided down an aluminum chute from the kitchen. Lori put it on a Styrofoam plate and slid it across the counter to Danielle.

"Are you crazy? Of course I don't miss it. How could anyone in her right mind miss all that noise, all those sticky little hands and faces," Danielle said. She sighed. "I even had to miss my manicure last week. Look at my nails, they're still a wreck from those kids," Danielle said, holding out her hands for Lori's inspection. "I missed a great sale at Facades too. Luckily, one of the saleswomen put some things aside for me. I've been having a wonderful time this afternoon—exercising, shopping, treating myself *right* for a change."

Lori glanced at her. Danielle didn't sound very convincing. "Sounds great," Lori said.

"Right—then why in the world am I not having any fun?" Danielle asked Lori. "I mean, I always feel great hanging out at the mall all afternoon. But for some reason, the more I do it today, the worse I feel."

Without realizing it, Danielle began to pour out her heart to Lori, talking with her just as she did when they were as close as sisters. Danielle explained that all she'd been thinking about the last week was getting back into circulation. But that afternoon she had realized that, compared to watching the kids at the day-care center, her life at the mall seemed shallow and almost boring.

Lori gave her cousin a sympathetic smile. She could never recall Danielle acting like this. Usually, the only thing that could get Danielle upset was a less than perfect haircut, or a guy she had a crush on not asking her out. And either event was *extremely* rare. Lori didn't know what to say to make her cousin feel better.

"I guess working at the center, you learned a lot more than just how to watch little kids."

"Like, there's more to life than getting your nails polished?" Danielle asked with a slight smile.

"You said it, Dani—I didn't." Lori laughed.

"Maybe you should think of volunteering there on a regular basis. I mean, if you miss it so much."

"Hmmm—I don't know. Doing it to help my grade was one thing. And even though the kids were fun, I don't know if I want all that responsibility." Danielle sighed. "Well, I guess I'll think about it. See you around," she said, taking her soda and taco.

"See you," Lori answered. She knew she'd failed to cheer Danielle up. But sometimes when a person has a lot to figure out, she reflected, nothing anyone can say will help. Danielle had to work things out for herself.

Lori was thinking of the mistake she had made with Nick. She would do anything in the world to go back and live Saturday all over again. Lori knew now that she would have made a different choice. A choice that was true to her heart and not to her head.

Danielle nibbled on her taco, then tossed most of it in the trash. She decided that she might as well go home. The afternoon had been a total dud. She thought she had missed hanging out at the mall, but right then, she really missed being with all the kids at the center. The afternoon of indulging all her whims seemed pretty dull in comparison to their company.

"Hey, Red! Wait up!" Danielle heard Don's voice and turned to see him sauntering toward

her from across the mall, a large paper bag in
his hand. "I was downtown and stopped in at
the day-care center to say hi, but you weren't
there."

"I only had to work there for fifteen hours.
Just to improve my psych grade, remember?"
Danielle said.

"Well, why you did it doesn't matter." He
shrugged. "Not when you think of how much
you helped the kids and how happy you made
them."

"Oh, Don, don't be so nice to me. I didn't
even take care of them right yesterday. I wasn't
such a great volunteer—"

"You weren't, huh? Well, I just met about a
dozen little people and a teacher who disagree
with you. As a matter of fact, when I got there,
the kids had just finished making you a surprise
and Miss Harper asked if I would deliver it."

"A surprise? For me?" For the first time all
day, Danielle's eyes took on their usual bright
glow. "What kind of surprise?"

"It's all in here," Don replied with a smile.
He handed over the paper bag.

Danielle peeked inside. It was filled with the
children's drawings. She pulled a few pieces
out and saw that all of them were of her. Some
even showed her and Garbo. On the bottom of
the stack she found a letter that each of the kids
had signed their name to. Written in crayon,
the big red print said, "Dear Danielle, We miss

you and hope you will come back and play with us again!"

Danielle thought she was going to cry. Here she was moping around all afternoon, thinking she had been such a failure. But it just wasn't so. Feeling positively jubilant, she turned to Don with a radiant smile.

"Good news, I guess," he said, smiling back.

"The best! Thank you, Don, for bringing this to me. It's just about the most precious gift I've ever gotten!" Before Danielle thought twice about what she was doing, she threw her arms around Don and gave him a big hug.

Then she did think about it and pulled back, staring at him. Her heart was thumping and her knees were rubber.

"Hey, Red, remind me to have you thank me more often. I keep telling you we'd be good together," he said in a husky voice.

Collecting herself, Danielle said, "Dream on." She did turn back, though, as she ran for the exit, and said, "By the way, thanks!"

If she hurried, there was just barely enough time to get downtown to thank the children for all they'd given her.

CHAPTER FOURTEEN

Although Danielle was unaware of it, Lori had been watching the entire happy scene. Ernie had just told her she could go on a break. When Lori stepped outside Tio's she saw her cousin talking with Don James.

Lori watched as Danielle's bleak expression lit up and she gave Don a big hug. Then she stood staring at him before running off toward the exit. Lori didn't know what had made Danielle so happy, but she hoped it had something to do with the children from the day-care center—and Don.

Lori decided to take a walk around the mall. She was glad to see her cousin looking so happy, and only wished she could say the same for herself. She still was feeling down, and was afraid she'd forgotten how to smile. She had been crying herself to sleep the last three nights and had woken up every morning with swollen, puffy eyes. She tried not to think of Nick, but it was impossible. Every place she passed in the mall jogged a special memory for her.

They hadn't spoken or seen each other since the game on Saturday, but she promised herself the night before that she wouldn't call him again. Her friends kept telling her to give him time. But Lori was sure that if he hadn't tried to see her by now, they would never get back together again. She had ruined everything.

Lori soon found herself at the entrance to the parking lot. Nick had kissed her in that very spot and told her that he thought she was the most wonderful girl he'd ever known. That was the night he had taken Danielle to the Harvest Ball. Lori had been devastated. But despite Danielle's considerable charms, Nick couldn't get Lori off his mind. After he left the dance early, he returned to the mall and waited for Lori to finish work. He hadn't been able to wait another day to tell her that she was the only girl for him.

Reliving those happy moments, Lori felt as if she would cry. She leaned up against the wall and hid her face in her hands. All dreams must end sooner or later, she thought sadly.

All of a sudden the sound of angry voices echoed through the parking lot. Lori couldn't see where the shouts were coming from at first, but she could hear what they were saying.

"Don't try to escape, Hobart! We want to talk

to you," one angry voice shouted. "You better have a reason for losing that game on Saturday."

"You betrayed us! You threw the game on purpose!" someone else called.

Lori ran toward the voices and saw Nick standing beside his car, surrounded by a few students from Atwood. They were tightening their circle around Nick and were so intent on him that no one even saw Lori.

Although Nick was facing them bravely, Lori saw his face go pale. Her stomach twisted in a giant knot. These guys had been waiting for him and were going to gang up on him—six against one! Nick was going to get beaten up, and there was no one around to help him. Lori considered running back to the mall for a security guard, but by then, she thought, it might be too late.

"Time to take your lumps, quarterback. Too bad you fumbled that pass, because now we're going to fumble your face," one guy sneered.

"Hey, I know what you think, but it just isn't so," Nick yelled over their angry voices. "You guys think it's so easy out there on the field. Why don't you try it sometime? See what you can do against hundreds of pounds of Merivale linemen."

"Shut your stupid face, Hobart. Before I shut it for you." Another boy stepped up to Nick and shoved him back hard against his car. Nick nearly fell to the ground, but caught himself just in time. "We heard you threw the Merivale game because of your girlfriend. She goes to Merivale, doesn't she?"

Lori gasped. It was all *her* fault! These kids were after Nick because of her! She had to stop them. Without a second thought, Lori left her cover and pushed into the middle of the circle.

"You're wrong!" she shouted. "Nick didn't throw that game. And he certainly didn't throw it for me. I swear it! It wasn't like that at all."

"Yeah, sure." The boy who had pushed Nick sneered at her. "Tell us another one, Blondie."

"Lori! Get away from here!" Nick yelled at her. "I can handle this. These creeps don't care who gets hurt."

"Your boyfriend is right. You'd better get out of the way, before you get hurt too," another one warned her. "I mean it."

He tugged on her arm, but Lori had the advantage of surprise and unexpectedly yanked her arm free. Instantly she assumed a karate fighting stance—her feet and arms set. "I have to warn you I'm a black belt in karate," she said deliberately.

There was a long, tense moment. Lori could hear her own heart pounding wildly in her chest. She didn't look at Nick, although she could sense him beside her tensing his muscles, ready to fight. "Go ahead," she said, challenging the kid. "Try me. Make my day!"

None of the six guys could really believe that

she was a black belt, but no one really wanted to hurt her either.

Slowly they all backed up as Nick stepped out after them. When they were out of sight, Nick turned and stared openmouthed at Lori.

"You're not *really* a karate expert, are you?" he said with a smile.

"Nope. But I *do* have two little brothers. I know all the moves from them."

"But, Lori, no one says those lines, except guys in the movies."

"Well, it worked, didn't it?" she said and stood looking at him.

And then they started to laugh—great rolling floods of laughter that soon had them doubled over and gasping for air. Tears ran down both their cheeks, and they slid to the ground, leaning against Nick's Camaro and holding their sides.

Never had Lori laughed so hard—and it wasn't just because of her karate moves. The laughter released the tension that had been building for the past few weeks.

Finally the great belly rolls subsided, and they both stood up, panting. Both occasionally hiccuped and snickered. Then, Nick turned to Lori and said, "Lori, you really are the best. I know why I care about you so much." He moved toward her and then stopped himself.

"Do you really?" she asked finally. "Care about me?"

He nodded. "Lori, I want us to be together again. The way it used to be—" he said sadly.

"Then why did you want to break up?" she asked.

"I didn't really," he said simply.

"But what about what you said after the game?" Lori reminded him. "I kept calling you, but you didn't call back—"

"I was just upset. I was mad at myself—never really mad at you. You were just there." He moved closer and placed his hands on her shoulders. "Please, Lori, can we try again?" He shook his head. "I was wrong to try to force you to make such an impossible choice. I see that now. You didn't make me fumble that ball. I did it all by myself. Can you forgive me for being such a jerk?"

"You're not a jerk," Lori replied and started to cry as she walked into his arms, leaning against him.

Nick finally smiled and held her tight. "Hey, beautiful, if I say I'm a jerk, I'm a jerk. Got it? Or do you want to argue some more?"

"Never," Lori replied, smiling through her tears.

Then Nick lifted her chin up, and the look in his eyes made Lori feel as if she were going to melt. She reached up and put her arms around his neck. And then she gave him a long and lingering kiss. It felt so right to be in Nick's arms again, so wonderfully right.

When their kiss finally ended, Nick hugged her tight and Lori rested her head against his chest. "There's something else I'm never going to do," Lori whispered.

"Hmm?" Nick looked down at her and dropped a small kiss on the tip of her nose. "Not wear a dumb Halloween mask anymore, I hope. Even if you're cruising around, trashing my school, I don't think you should hide this pretty face for a second."

"No, silly, I'm serious," Lori said. "Once you told me to let my heart decide what to do. But I was too dumb to see that you were right. From now on, I'm going to trust my feelings. Especially about you and me."

"From now on," Lori declared, "I'm going to stop playing games!"